SHADY ACRES
AND DARKER PLACES

STORIES BY

DOUG LANE

MIDNIGHT-TO-THREE PUBLISHING
HOUSTON, TX
2018

Published by Midnight-To-Three Publishing
Houston, TX

978-0-9895417-5-6 (limited edition hardcover)
978-0-9895417-3-2 (trade paperback)
978-0-9895417-4-9 (ebook)

"The Golem-Maker of Buchenwald" appeared online at *Abyss & Apex Magazine*, July 2016 •
"Good Bait", "Erin Beiber's Wild Ride" and "To The Devil, A Goat" appeared in *Seasons In The Abyss*, ed. by Jack Burton, Blood Bound Books, February 2011 • "The Sinking Tomb" appeared online at *Fiction365.com*, March 2013 • "The Last Ride of the Hole In The Well Gang" appeared in *Sugar & Rice #3*, October 2014 • "Dial 'C' For Consultant" appeared in *We Were Heroes*, ed. by Martin T. Ingram, Martinus Publishing, February 2016 • "The Jail In Shinjuku Ward" appeared online at *Pure Francis*, February 2009 • "Lorem Ipsum Donald" appeared in *Tales of the Unanticipated #31*, March 2014 • "Ark Of The Revenant" appeared in *The Midnight Diner 5.1*, January 2014 • "Fear #7" appeared online at *Stupefying Stories Showcase*, October 2016 • "Every Hero An Hombre, Every Wolf A Clown" appeared online at *The Saturday Evening Post*, February 2016 • "One Man's Famine" appeared in *Bards and Sages Quarterly*, October 2011 • "The Shaman In Relief" appeared in *Two In Left Field*, Midnight-to-Three Publishing, July 2013 • "Shady Acres" appeared online at *Pure Francis*, March 2009 • "The Trapdoor" appeared in *Blood Rites*, ed. by Marc Ciccarone, Blood Bound Books, January 2013 • "Tacklesmooches" appeared in *Tales of the Unanticipated #30*, Spring 2010 • "Physicians' Ball" appeared online at *Pure Francis*, January 2011 • "In Days Of Auld Cheil's Crime" appeared online at douglasjlane.com, December 2016 • "Bobby Boxster In Eight Measures" appeared in *Washington City Paper*, January 2015 • "Withering" appeared in *Beyond Imagination*, September 2015. All stories have been revised from their original publications.

Originally published as a limited edition hardcover.

First trade paperback publication November, 2018

Contents

Glimpsed In Shadow (An Introduction)   IX
The Golem-Maker of Buchenwald   1
Good Bait   13
The Sinking Tomb   17
The Last Ride of the Hole In The Well Gang   23
Dial 'C' For Consultant   35
The Jail in Shinjuku Ward   47
Lorem Ipsum Donald   51
Ark of the Revenant   63
Fear #7   75
Every Hero An Hombre, Every Wolf A Clown   79
To The Devil, A Goat   91
One Man's Famine   95
The Shaman In Relief   99
Shady Acres   115
Erin Beiber's Wild Ride   117
The Trapdoor   121
Tacklesmooches   133
Physicians' Ball   145
In Days of Auld Cheil's Crime   149
Bobby Boxster in Eight Measures   159
Withering   167
How The Sausage Was Made (A Postscript)   171

DEDICATION

She supplied me with books,
encouraged my interest in writing,
was one of my first constant readers.

I know, I know. It's what moms do.

But there wouldn't be a book
for you–or for me–without her.

For my mom,
Patricia Lane
(1946 - 2017)

GLIMPSED IN SHADOW
(AN INTRODUCTION)

What's in the dark?

You've caught glimpses of things from the corner of your eye, had that shiver in the shade that can't be explained as a simple absence of light. There are shadows, and then there's darkness within them–places of curiosity and fear, of wonder and melancholy.

We're compelled to check them out, even when the flesh prickles and the urge is to back away. We can't help it. We're only human. Most of the time.

This collection flies in the face of convention. They (the mystical, all-seeing **They**) say a collection should be one thing–all SF, all fantasy, all horror, all whatever flavor. They say it needs to be this way if you're going to find the intended audience. There's probably some truth to that. The marketing of the film BUCKAROO BANZAI was all blind men and elephants: was it an adventure? A comedy? Satire?

Pulp homage? It didn't fit in the box, and so it couldn't be sold like things in a box.

To me, stories are stories. The great Ray Bradbury had no qualms about putting a journey to Mars alongside the examination of a murder alongside a celebration of summer running, all within the same covers. He simply told stories. Genre is as much a tool as tense, person, grammar. It lets you frame an argument. The trail rider trying to round up stray cattle and the starship captain trying to account for all the life-pods are basically in the same pickle; the 'who-what-where' comes down to how best to probe the main character's conflicts.

This book contains tales that range from fantasy to horror, with excursions in the supernatural, light science fiction, and straight-up literature. Their lengths vary widely, as do their moods. This is simply the way I tell stories. As this may be our first date, I didn't want to give you the wrong impression.

But they *do* have a common thread: all of them wind a path through darker places, whether those trips are fantastical (raising a golem), horrific (literally falling apart), whimsical (breaking a curse), or grounded in the real-world (finding yourself after addiction). Darkness is merely gradients, the dance between the angle and amount of light and the size of the obstacle. Some shadows, you can leap.

Others, you're bound to fall into.

I wonder what you'll glimpse if you do.

Doug Lane
October, 2018

SHADY ACRES
AND DARKER PLACES

THE GOLEM-MAKER OF
BUCHENWALD

"WE WERE TOLD YOU can create a golem." The man in the suit flicks ash from a thin black cigarette into the ash tray.

Gerstmann turns from the TV behind the bar–Mayor Koch making proclamations about the ongoing city newspaper strike–and studies the man. Sheffer's card says he's a director of cultural affairs for the Israeli Minister of the Interior. His suit makes the bar look cheap.

Gerstmann sips his gimlet. Frowns. Too much lime juice. "I don't do that anymore."

"But you *are* Ira Gerstmann?"

"One of them."

"Born in 1934 in Erfurt, Germany to Bernard and Ruth Gerstmann."

"Friends called him Bernie."

"Your father died in the camps, but your mother was

liberated and emigrated to the United States with you."

"And her sister Miriam. There was also a schnauzer. A most unpleasant dog."

"Then you *are* the golem-maker of Buchenwald."

Gerstmann dismisses the notion with a wave. "There was no golem at Buchenwald. Camp resistance had no need of one. They had guns and patience and a short-wave radio. All the magic they needed."

"Men who were there say they saw it rise."

"I'm a man who was there. The only thing that rose in Buchenwald was a cheer, when the Americans came through the gate. You know how legends build. They begin as pebbles at the summit. Those fall. More join them, and more, until they beget an avalanche that buries the foot of the mountain. Try finding the original pebbles in the rubble."

Sheffer's lips hint at a smile. "Then tell me the truth behind the legend."

"The truth? They gave a hyperactive ten-year-old something on which to focus his energy, so the guards didn't stave in his head." Gerstmann has already said more about Buchenwald in a half-hour than he has in the decade preceding. "Much later, I successfully raised a golem. Once or twice. Assistance to old women or rabbis with pest problems. But as I said, I don't do that anymore."

Sheffer takes a drag. Smoke drifts from his scowl. The story has fallen short of his expectation. Gerstmann hears Bubbe Nussbaum in his head. *Expectations are like eyelids, Ira. Everyone has a couple, and they can't see past them.* The woman was a Polish iron-work made flesh. She was sent to Ravensbrück early in the war, reduced to ghosts and memory. Gerstmann cannot recall her face now without a photographic prompt, of which there remain only two. Two more than many.

"Why not?" Sheffer asks.

Gerstmann thinks of five reasons, broken-necked and splashed across the front page of the Post. His stomach churns

2

anew. "How did you find me?"

"Ben Kastner works with my office. He told me you come here. He says you attended *mesivta* together."

"True enough." Gerstmann makes a silent vow to rap Ben Kastner in the mouth the next time he sees him, for talking out of school.

"Plus I've seen pictures at the Ministry of the golem you raised for Irene Rosen."

"Pictures?"

"Her rabbi found it in her basement after she died. It was there with an envelope containing your correspondence on the matter."

Gerstmann wonders if the woman simply died before she could destroy it, or kept it as some kind of memento. He feels naked. "What became of it?"

"It was inert. After he photographed it, the rabbi destroyed the form. Dust to dust."

Gerstmann takes another sip and pushes the glass away, the drink devolving as quickly as his control of the conversation. "What need does the Minister of the Interior of the State of Israel have for a golem?"

Sheffer lifts a briefcase from beside his chair. He pops brass latches. "I trust you will keep what I'm about to tell you a secret."

"I'm 43, unmarried, and unemployed. Who would I tell?"

Sheffer sets a folder on the table and pushes it across. "We need someone to protect Avner Wollman."

Gerstmann opens the folder. He flips through a series of newspaper articles and fuzzy photocopies as Sheffer narrates. "Wollman is a German Jew. An Auschwitz survivor. His testimony helped tie the noose around the neck of Franz Hössler at the Belsen Trial. Heard of him?"

Gerstmann shakes his head. If he doesn't recognize the name, the story is familiar. He's incapable of remembering all the people who have testified at some time to something done

3

in Germany or Poland or the dozen other countries that had camps, a fraternity chartered by history.

"He's a cultural treasure," Sheffer continues. "A writer, photographer and poet. He started by self-publishing his own experiences. He was also one of the first survivors to return to the camps after the war to document them. He recorded oral histories of their inmates, as well as people in the towns nearby. He's highly regarded as an outspoken champion of human rights and an enemy of war criminals. He is thus very important to Israel."

Gerstmann skims pages. Samples of the man's work. Interviews. Lecture transcripts. Photographs of places for which Gerstmann's memory needs no prompt. "Where is he now?"

"Rio de Janeiro. He went there in 1974 on vacation and decided to stay. Keeps to himself. I'd call it retirement, but he still publishes the occasional op-ed."

"And from who or what does he need protection?"

"For four years, Wollman flew under the radar. But in the last few months, people have begun harassing him. There are individuals down there still sympathetic to the Nazis–expatriate German nationals, Holocaust deniers, that ilk. Wollman doesn't want a thug with a gun. He thinks that invites trouble." Sheffer flips to the back of the folder, to a color snapshot of Wollman sitting at a table outside a cafe. The man's face is old, creased, hard. His gaze bores up from the image, annoyance at being photographed.

"You think a golem is the answer?"

Sheffer points at the photo. "He does. The Minister thinks they're a fairy tale."

"And you?"

Sheffer shrugs. "I'm a little more open to the notion of such things."

Gerstmann sighs. "I don't *do* this anymore."

"I have three men on my list. The other two are both

elderly rabbis, only rumored to have raised golems. You, I've seen proof. I'd prefer you." He takes another drag, the tip of his cigarette rage red, then fading. "You would be well-compensated for your work. Monetary payment for time and effort. A personal letter of thanks from the Minister of the Interior. I also understand you've been unemployed for six months."

Gerstmann's tone cuts. "Does the Ministry also know my brand of toothpaste and my shoe size?"

"We can also offer you a job. The Ministry maintains an office in lower Manhattan, if you don't mind clerical work."

Gerstmann studies the man for some sign of mirth. All he sees through the haze of cigarette smoke is grim determination.

"I need to think about it," Gerstmann says, with no real intention to give it another thought.

~o~

Gerstmann takes the D train to Bay Parkway in south Brooklyn and walks home. The autumn night is crisp. Winter is going to sting. As he passes other homes in the row, he sees his house is dark. He always leaves the porch light and a living room lamp illuminated.

He steps onto the small porch and sees the notice on the door. The Con Ed logo is more festive than the words that leap out at him in the glow of the street light: "service disconnected," "account past due," other utility company hate-speak toward the unemployed. He stuffs the notice in his pocket and unlocks the door.

"Yeah, the power jockeys were here," a voice says behind Gerstmann. He turns to see Milkin, his neighbor for the last ten years, on the adjacent porch. Milkin's a busybody, his eyes always watching, his lips crowded with probing questions. "Money troubles?"

"No. Just a crossed payment. A miscommunication."

"Oh." Milkin pauses. "Because it seems like you've been out of work for a while." He stops again, as if the words need to queue in his mouth. "You know, my younger son has a lot of pull at his firm. They respect his opinion. He worked on that Son of Sam thing. I can ask him to float your resume to their accounting department."

"Thanks, Milkin. I'll let you know."

"I mean, it won't be easy. You don't find a lot of guys your age just starting at law firms. What are you, 50?"

"I'm 43, but thanks for the extra birthdays. Goodnight, Milkin." Gerstmann enters the house and closes his door.

~o~

Gerstmann sits on the old wooden stool in his basement, candlelight flickering on the walls, the porcelain tub, his workbench. He sets aside his bowl of cereal. He uncorks a bottle of Kentucky bourbon and pours two fingers worth into a clear glass. He rocks the glass between his hands, the bourbon making confused currents.

He peers into the shadows and thinks about the non-golem of Buchenwald. Remembers its smooth face and broad shoulders, large arms and hands, feet that could have crushed a guard with the casual flex of a knee. The situation was exactly as he described to Sheffer: the other prisoners, the ones who adopted him after his father was marched off and never returned, conceived it to occupy the boy's mind. The appeal to his imagination was successful enough–Gerstmann had seen his grandfather animate such a figure once, when Gerstmann was five–but the form was never completed. The arrival of the American Third Army rendered the point moot. But the act of forming the figure, the possibility of such magic by his hands, took root in Gerstmann's young mind.

The expectation was always that Gerstmann would follow the rabbinical path of his father and grandfather. He surrendered short of his formal *semikhah*. It was a huge scandal in Rego Park in 1955. He was pulled instead by the mystic.

He wonders sometimes if that first success, a small man of clay he designed as an experiment, was where he laid a normal life–wife, children, a respected position in the community, a place of faith and peace–upon a sacrificial altar.

One or two, he told Sheffer. The actual number of golems raised would stun the man. Helpers, protectors, guards, tuned to the needs of the individual served. Gerstmann took pride in each of them, and might have gone on making them if not for Benny Getty.

Gerstmann animated a helper for Mrs. Getty in 1967, when glaucoma stole her eyesight. It was a favor to his mother. Mrs. Getty was one of her first friends in New York after the war.

Getty's son Benny, a small time hood fresh off a stint at Rikers, arrived home one day in 1968 to discover his mother's helper. Unable to keep his nose clean, and well-read for a hood, Benny re-tasked the golem to be his enforcer in a protection racket.

In the end, Benny wound up in Bellevue for the people the golem killed, if only because no one accepted that a pile of dust in his mother's home had ever been animate enough to break the necks of five goombahs at a Brooklyn warehouse, no matter how many times Benny said it.

The broken bodies, splayed across the pages of the New York Post, were too much for Gerstmann. He set aside his tools and swore off the craft, gnawing guilt in his gut. He hadn't sculpted a human form since.

Gerstmann drinks his bourbon and mulls Sheffer's offer. Like most bad decisions, it's more attractive by candlelight.

When he finishes his drink, Gerstmann walks upstairs. Con Ed may have forsaken him, but Ma Bell, that great telephonic bubbe, hasn't. He dials Sheffer's number.

~o~

Clay dredged from Gravesend Bay is purified in the deep porcelain tub, liquified and strained to remove sediments. It takes three days to clarify enough for the form.

The body begins as a long oval. Under Gerstmann's hands, the shape emerges, molded to Sheffer's specifications: "Muscular. Compact. A towering figure will only draw attention to Wollman. Anglo features. Nondescript."

Before he details the face, Gerstmann writes in Hebrew on the back of the color photo of Wollman from Sheffer's folder. SHAMAR. Keep. Protect. He layers clay over the image to form the forehead, the golem's mission hard-coded.

When the figure is done, Gerstmann selects detail pieces from the apothecary chest along the basement wall. Glass eyes of azure blue. Strands of coffee-colored hair woven from silk. Fish scales trimmed into fingernails. It's all part of the verisimilitude. Wollman's golem needs to walk alongside men.

When the detail work is complete and the golem sewn into appropriate garments, Gerstmann begins the incantation prayers. They are long, involved, precise. They demand perfect focus. If he stumbles or falters, he must begin again. Gerstmann surprises himself by not fumbling a syllable of the litany.

He finishes by carving all but the final stroke of the final character of the Hebrew word for Truth–EMETH–on the golem's forehead. When it reaches Rio de Janeiro, Sheffer will complete the word to animate the golem. Gerstmann's never left animation to someone else. It's like entrusting a child to a stranger's care.

Four men and a truck arrive the next day, dispatched by Sheffer. They are baby-faced. Gerstmann worries they will be careless. Instead, they crate the golem with slow, deliberate movements, as if handling sweating dynamite. Gerstmann doesn't engage them in small talk.

They load the golem and pile into the truck. The driver hands Gerstmann an envelope. His compensation: a cream-colored check. A signed letter of thanks from the Minister. Directions to the Ministry office downtown, and a welcome letter from the hiring manager. Paid in full.

Gerstmann watches the truck's retreat. He looks at the check, then his watch. He has enough time before the bank closes to start getting back on his feet.

~o~

Gerstmann's boots crunch snow underfoot, the sidewalk uncleared. The February wind tugs at his coat. He contemplates the joy of sleeping late on Saturday.

As Gerstmann tops his porch steps, Milkin emerges next door without a coat. He sips a Schlitz. Gerstmann wonders if the old man wants pneumonia. "Gerstmann. Beautiful night, huh?" The words are slurred around the edges.

Gerstmann stomps to clear his boots. "You've started your weekend early."

Milkin waves a fresh can at Gerstmann. "Drink with me, neighbor. Drink to life. To justice. To the blessed end of an era."

"What's in your bonnet?"

"The butcher is dead. Down in Sao Paolo." Milkin takes a long swig of his beer. "My older son called this afternoon. It's all hush-hush, but he had to tell me. They got him. God is good, Gerstmann. God is *good*."

"Who got whom?" Although standing on his porch, Gerstmann feels like he's lost in the snow.

"Mengele. That murdering Nazi cow. They've been watching him for years. Argentina, Paraguay, Brazil–they could never touch him. The official story will be drowning. They're gonna let him be buried under his fake name, 'discover' he's dead later. No headstone, no grave to worship at."

Gerstmann gapes. "Mengele? But... who? They *who*?"

Milkin takes another swallow. "The Mossad. My older son is a station chief in South America. Has his finger on the pulse. He figured they'd take the butcher alive some day, like Eichmann, but I guess it got ugly. He said Mengele's head was damn near screwed off his shoulders."

Milkin says more, but Gerstmann doesn't hear. He steps inside, closes his door. His eyes are full of dead goombahs in Brooklyn again. He retrieves Sheffer's card from the study. Dials the number, wondering how close Sao Paolo is to Rio.

~o~

The next afternoon, Sheffer stands in Gerstmann's dining room. He refuses coffee or tea. He declines a seat, put out. Gerstmann wonders why the man even bothered to make the trip.

"Is Avner Wollman real?" Gerstmann asks.

Sheffer shakes his head. "The entire folder was a prop for your benefit."

"Who was in the picture?"

"He was a Sao Paolo local. A drunk. Nobody. But he had the element we needed: Mengele didn't like him. Mengele thought he looked Jewish. He swung at the guy for fun. Old bastard. It gave us an opportunity. We created Avner Wollman."

The room is so quiet, Gerstmann hears his watch ticking. "You used me."

"We were directed to be hands off. I needed something outside the box. An unconventional weapon. One you knew how to build."

"I don't animate golems as weapons. They're intended to protect. To preserve. Not to destroy!"

10

"No?" Sheffer leans over a chair. "Let me ask you: if ten year old Ira Gerstmann had been capable of finishing the task, what would his golem have done to the Buchenwald guards? Talked them into surrender? Reasoned with them? No."

"I had no chance of success."

"I'm speaking to intent, not ability. It would have maimed and ripped and torn and crushed and killed those guards, to the point of its own destruction, to protect the people in that camp."

Gerstmann glares. His body shakes. His voice fails him.

"Tell me, Gerstmann. If I'd approached you with the real reason I wanted your expertise, would you have told me 'no'?"

Gerstmann begins to answer. He remembers Buchenwald, the stench of death and dying and fear. His affirmation dies on his tongue, unspoken.

His silence pulls Sheffer's mouth into a smug pucker. "If it makes you feel better, the culmination of your life's work has the thanks of a grateful nation." He leaves through the side door.

Gerstmann listens to Sheffer's car drive away. He begins to weep. Not from being The Mossad's dupe. Nor for Mengele. Never for Mengele. He might even be share-a-Schlitz-with-Milkin pleased the bastard is dead.

He weeps because he cannot bring himself to speak truth to Sheffer's question, even to himself.

When he's done weeping, Gerstmann descends to his basement. He peers around his workshop. He thinks about the golem, provoked by Mengele's swing at a Sao Paolo barfly into twisting Mengele's head from his shoulders.

Gerstmann steps to the corner. The wooden handle of the rusted sledgehammer is rough in his grip. His first swing tears an irreparable hole in the side of the old porcelain tub.

—o—

GOOD BAIT

The red drum were running strong, and the one Tully hooked was a leviathan. Pull, crank, let it run, pull, crank–he danced the way his father taught him, wrestled the fish out of the water and up as it thrashed its body. As he maneuvered a net around it and heaved it over the rail, he eyeballed the thing. Fifty pounds? Not a record, but damned fine for April.

"Good bait," Harteford said beside him, admiring the fish. It was the third Tully had pulled that morning. Almost limit. "What are you using?"

Tully could feel the simmering envy in Harteford, whose hooks might as well have been snorkeling. "Do-it-yourself," he said. "Mullet, mackerel, a little shrimp, bloodworm, other bits." It was only half-true; no honor among fishermen where tricks of the trade were concerned. "If it keeps working like this, I might have a chance in competition this year. Take a prize or two. Maybe pull a record."

They stood at the end of the pier, the waves a watery

heartbeat against the pilings. Despite the warmth and the cloudless sky, they were alone. Tully liked slow days. Too many amateurs clogged the pier once it got hot, tourists with no sense for angling. The bait shop kept a nurse on call for dealing with unwanted hand piercings.

"D'ja hear McKlusky's missing?" Tully asked.

Harteford played out a little more line. "Damn. Really?"

"Yeah. Marion says he went up to New York to do some ice fishing in December. Didn't say where. Didn't come back. Cops are still looking."

"Damn," Harteford said again. "McKlusky sure knows how to catch a fish."

The red drum in the cooler, Tully dipped a hand into his bucket and fished out another chunk of bait. "Sure does." The barbed ends of his hooks slid silently into the flesh. It oozed from the perforations. He cast the line. Sinker and bait plunked into the waves twenty yards off.

"I hope nothing bad happened to him," Harteford said. "Though it might be easier for a guy to win a contest without him around."

Tully shot him a sideways glance. "The man could be at the bottom of a lake somewhere, and you're worried about a bass tournament?"

"I didn't mean anything by it."

"That's pretty callous. Marion is worried sick."

"Jeez, I'm sorry." Harteford sounded more sorry he'd aired the thought, not the content. "It's just that he's been winning the thing for twenty years."

Harteford wasn't seasonal, but he'd only been a resident for a few years. He hadn't spent the two decades the rest of them had, battling McKlusky, his secret fishing spot, year after year of prize bass. Tully and the other old-timers had reason for frustration. Coming from Harteford, it seemed unduly competitive.

They fished in silence a while longer before Harteford

14

packed up. "Hope McKlusky turns up," he said by way of goodbye, annoyance in his voice. Tully listened to Harteford's footfalls as the man receded down the long pier. Then Tully's reel began to turn. Pull, crank, let it run, pull, crank. Whatever it was, it felt big. Record big. Tully could feel it fighting him in the undercurrent. The line pulled taut. He gave it slack, muscled the pole, could feel whatever was down there was turning, giving up.

The line snapped.

Tully sighed and reeled in the slack. He tied a new hook and sinker onto the ragged end of the wet, white line. He plucked a fresh piece of bait from the bucket and skewered it on the hook. The glint of sunlight off something in the bucket caught his eye. He wondered how he'd missed it.

The drum might like something shiny, he thought.

He tied McKlusky's wedding band to the line and cast the freshly baited hook into the rolling sea.

—o—

The Sinking Tomb

THE GREAT SHIP GROANED. It was tilting fore and listing to port, the creak of its young hull joined with the spitting hiss of signal rockets fired from its upper deck, death-cries in the stillness. The lower decks were filled with water, gripped by the cold, hands of the North Atlantic.

The failing vessel's passengers milled with purpose on the deck in the chilled night air, but they were restrained. No rueful musings or rent garments, no bartering for miracles with the empty heavens, none of the chaos commensurate with certain death. There was commotion, certainly. It was a loud and distressed crowd, but with a strange order. Disruptions were scatter-shot: a stray scream, a bark of orders from the ship's officers, or the occasional coward trying to fight his way in front of the women and children.

Jacques Futrelle took in the scene. A journalist and writer folded within the news, he felt a twinge of annoyance. He was never going to set this surreal evening down on paper. Titanic, felled by an iceberg. He wanted a byline, not to be listed with the casualties.

He waved to his wife, May. She was quiet aboard the collapsible lifeboat, waiting for it to be filled and lowered. *Soon*, he thought. He did nothing to upset the portrait of confidence with which he'd gotten her seated, the reassurances he would be on his own boat, right behind her into the Atlantic. She was no fool. She could see how his life would end. Yet he read in her expression a need for the lie from his lips, some hope braced against her certainty that she was going to survive him.

Futrelle needed only to keep the facade in place until he was beyond her sight. But the sea was no match for the tears on her cheeks, and the sight of them cut deeper than the inability to capture the scene of the ordered mob on the deck, jockeying for position to game the ghoulish lottery into which the iceberg had cast them all.

"Futrelle," a voice said. Futrelle turned from May to find John Jacob Astor IV beside him. He'd crossed paths with Astor several times during the voyage, heard his tales of invention, of real estate deals in Manhattan, of his service in Cuba. Astor was 47, ten years Futrelle's senior, and one of the wealthiest men on the planet. It was hard to not picture him as a massive Morgan dollar in a bowler and Oxfords. Shaped by life experience, Astor carried himself well in disaster. In his suit, hat, topcoat and gloves, he might have been passing on his way to the opera. But there was a touch of frost in the man's meticulously groomed moustache, a resignation in his eyes. He held an open cigarette case out to Futrelle. The golden tray glinted in the lights of the deck. "Join me."

"Colonel. Thank you." Futrelle's chilly fingers fumbled at extracting one of the rolls of tobacco. When Futrelle had it in hand, Astor struck a match. He lighted Futrelle's cigarette first, then his own. He closed the case with a crocodile snap and pocketed it.

The long drag on the cigarette warmed Futrelle inside. He

turned back to May and smiled at her, reinforcing the great lie. "I watched your bride's departure," he told Astor. Her lifeboat had been beside the one in which May was seated, lowered from the ship ten minutes before.

Astor scowled. "It was less dignified than I would have liked." Madeline Astor had wailed and begged and pleaded with her husband to join her in the lifeboat, to not leave her, to not send her down to the sea alone. Four times, he'd stepped aboard the small vessel, still in its davits, in an attempt to settle her. With great reluctance, Astor then asked permission of the officer in charge to accompany her. To his credit, when the officer turned him away, Astor did not offer to buy or barter his way back to her side. He accepted his fate as a gentleman. He soothed his wife's anguish and the boat was lowered.

"She's a young woman and a new bride in a terrible circumstance," Futrelle said. "Love is a natural balm to fear."

"Your wife seemed reluctant as well."

The crew began to lower the lifeboat carrying May. Futrelle nodded a reassurance to her. "I thought at first I would have to knock her out and dump her aboard like a sack of oats."

They smoked in silence as the crew loaded the next boat. Then Astor said, "You know, I've occasioned to read a number of your tales. Enjoyable diversions."

"Oh, well. Thank you, Colonel." Futrelle's view of his wife was obstructed by the ship's rail and bulkhead. Despite Astor's companionship, Futrelle felt a profound and sudden aloneness. "That is most gracious. I wouldn't have taken a man in your position as a reader of such amusements."

"Stories fill the narrow spaces left by business and travel. And sometimes, man needs a diversion."

"Indeed." Futrelle watched two crewmen fight back a younger man determined to push his way aboard one of the remaining lifeboats. The larger of the sailors hit the man open handed. The young man fell to the deck, stunned, eyes open

19

and unseeing.

"Tell me, Futrelle: how do you think your man would work his way out of this predicament?" Astor asked.

Futrelle stared at him. "Excuse me. My man?"

"The logician. Van Dusen. The Thinking Machine. How would he apply his vast store of logic to an escape from Titanic?"

Futrelle was silent. He'd given little thought on this voyage to Augustus S. F. X. Van Dusen, the fiercely logical scientist and problem-solver at the heart of much of Futrelle's fiction. He'd been writing other things. He'd recently finished a novel around a criminal named The Hawk. The character was still flitting around the edges of his imagination, whispering in his ear. Futrelle enjoyed writing Van Dusen, putting the character over a barrel and then figuring both of their ways out of the scrape, but what did he matter at a time like this?

"This is beyond the Van Dusen's purview," Futrelle said. "It's a better question for Harry Houdini."

A rumble shook the bowels of the ship. A door in the bulkhead nearby opened and two men with soot covering their blank expressions stepped on deck. They walked without purpose, a pair of ganders meandering aft.

"A diversion, sir," Astor said. "It will pass the time." He paused. "Please."

Futrelle looked from the dirty crewmen to Astor. If Astor felt fear, it was locked away as well as the commodities he traded. And yet, in the millionaire's eyes Futrelle saw a yearning for something to hold onto, not unlike the one in May's. Whatever had separated them when they boarded in Southampton–privilege, experience, wealth–had been torn away by the iceberg. They were, as the late Stephen Crane once described it, all together in the open boat.

"All right, then," Futrelle said, and slipped into Van Dusen's skin. "The ship is not unlike a cell, with the added peril of gradual submersion in freezing water. The most logical opportunity would have been to make one's way from the ship to the iceberg. While frigid, it is far easier to survive several hours in the night air in heavy clothing, clinging to an island of ice until rescue, than to be consumed by the unrelenting cold and wet weight of the sea."

"But the iceberg is gone," Astor said. "Passed in the night."

"Indeed. We did not run aground, but merely struck the thing a glancing blow. Only the most prescient aboard might have availed themselves of the opportunity to transfer to the more seaworthy vessel." Futrelle watched the crewmen filling the first of the final two lifeboats. Their pace had quickened. "In this situation, the physical world demonstrates certain truths. Paramount among them is this: without regard for material, a ship breached as ours will sink."

"We bear witness to such." Astor waved a hand towards the bow, closer now to the ocean's surface. Ash from the tip of his cigarette fluttered through the air.

"However, much of the vessel is still constructed of the nautical mainstay of centuries: wood. As reinforced by the lifeboats, the mandate for survival is that one need only remain out of the frigid water. Afloat."

"A raft," Astor said.

"Precisely. Not unlike something Huckleberry Finn and his slave friend Jim might have lashed together. Logs, rope, some pitch to hold it fast. It need not be sturdy enough to sail from Queenstown to New York. It need only support a man for several hours in calm waters, until rescue arrives." The list of the ship was growing more noticeable, but Futrelle felt compelled to conclude the thought. "If, at the time of the collision, one was to reject the notion that the White Star Line had made sufficient plans for disaster and take his fate into his own hands, there would have been plentiful time to manufacture a craft of moderate seaworthiness. The dining tables could have been transformed into a flotilla of such craft with the manpower available." He looked at Astor and managed a smile. "You might even have supplemented 'Colonel' with 'Commodore' for a time."

Astor returned the smile. He looked into the night sky. "I wrote a novel once. Did you know? A fanciful thing, a journey among the stars. Going back to a boy, I have always found the stars a comfort, even on those nights when my fortunes have soured or tragedy has stricken my family or myself." He looked back at Futrelle. His smile faded. "Tonight, they are high and brilliant, and as devoid of comfort as the darkness between them."

"I'm sorry I can offer you nothing else by way of hope, Colonel," Futrelle said. "Nature seems to have provided a predicament even the esteemed Thinking Machine would have had difficulty escaping."

"Not at all. In fact, just now you bested the stars at their usual game." Astor's expression grew hearty, determined. It was the look of a military man aware that his next battle was against Death itself, and his being unarmed only made it more sporting. He shook Futrelle's hand. "Godspeed, Futrelle."

Futrelle gave a nod. "Colonel Astor."

Astor walked along the canted deck, making his way forward, towards the bridge and the relentless churn of the Atlantic consuming the ship. Futrelle watched him go. Then he stepped to the rail, took a last puff of the cigarette, and flicked the spent roll over the side. He scanned the retreating lifeboats for a final glimpse of his beloved May.

—o—

The Last Ride of the Hole In The Well Gang

"Whiskey is for drinking;
water is for fighting over."

—unknown

There's a dead horse lying in the middle of the road in the headlights, so Pickney stops his truck.

United Water Authority guidelines say, "Don't stop." Pickney's guidelines say, "Don't die." He's on an uphill grade. Soft shoulder. Full load in the tanker. No guard rail. A gully full of roll-over to his right.

He's thinking it through when he hears a shell racked into a shotgun outside his door. The muzzle taps his window.

"Roll it down. Face away."

Don't die. Pickney complies.

He's blindfolded and pulled from the truck. His hands are zip-tied behind his back and he's forced to sit by the side of the road. He hears a truck approach.

His assailants connect hoses, begin a pump. Someone asks Pickney where he loaded, where he's headed, who's getting the shipment. He answers. Pickney's assailants retreat on the rumble of 340 horses.

When the highway patrol finds him and cuts him loose, Pickney confirms all 8,000 gallons of water in his tank are gone. On the windshield, a calling card sits under a wiper, black block letters on white card stock.

CHEERS,
THE HOLE IN THE WELL GANG

~o~

Five-strong, the gang sits around a table in an abandoned farmhouse, deciding the fate of the tanker in the barn.

Baker is human gristle, shaped by thirty years in drilling. It's Baker's crew.

Drake is the muscle, ten years younger, ten inches taller. He could take Baker in a fight, but prefers a full share and none of the decision-making.

Marco and Ramirez are all-purpose and don't complain. They'd rather go to jail than back to Mexico.

Then there's The Kid. He started life as Henry Hill but lied about his name (Walter Kidd) and home (Waco) and age (19) to get the job that led him here. Most heists he sits in the brush with a Remington 870 Express 12 gauge, loaded with seven ballistic bean-bags. The Kid thinks Baker has him on lookout with a crowd-control gun because he's only seventeen. The Kid is right.

Baker hangs up his cell. Points at Marco. "You and Drake take it to Freeport. The Casper Brothers are paying $3.80 a gallon to buy or two-to-one exchange, salt for farm grade, no questions."

"What's the agreement?"

"Cash for ten percent of the load, the rest in exchange. Bring the cash and 250 gallons in water allocation certificates back here. Distribute the rest of the certificates to these farms near Edna and Goliad." He hands Marco a list of addresses and amounts, farmers who don't know Christmas is coming early. "I'll text the next job site once I know it. Meet us there."

Marco nods and heads off to bunk. Drake asks Baker, "Why do you ask drivers all those questions?"

Baker waves a battered notebook, pages crammed with writing neat as a nun's. "I'm keeping track of Trevino's sins."

~o~

Trevino's aide, Abel, flags him outside the press room. "They hit the eastbound route again."

"How much this time?"

"Eight thousand, for the Beer Barons."

Augustus Trevino is the governor's appointee over the Unified Water Authority. His official title is Commissioner. The press calls him the Water Czar.

The Great Southern Drought is dug in like a tick, fifteen years deep. All the state's drought plans are busted. Schemes to survive on 45% of capacity are useless when the best reservoirs struggle to reach 25%.

In Year Ten, old regional squabbles over who pumped water from where blossomed into full-blown riots. After eleven people died in a clash over use of the Edwards Aquifer, the governor created the Unified Water Authority. A stroke of a pen, and the regional aquifer and reservoir managers were marching to the Water Czar's drum.

Whether Trevino makes the drought livable depends on who you ask. Big Business loves him, but it has big spigots. Municipalities enforce his residence rations, but it costs a fortune: thirsty people are sneaky people. The general public grumbles about three-minute showers and wants to know why the government isn't doing more.

Farmers are so low on his priority list, their feet dangle off the bottom. They have wastewater exchanges and rain capture systems and tax breaks on what they coax from the ground. What they don't have is water.

Their desire to be heard manifests in myriad ways. Cooler heads march on Austin and drum up public support at farmers markets. For others, frustration sows desperation. The rice growers who tried to kidnap the Water Czar four years ago may be welcomed as heroes when they get released from Coffield. The ones that survived the attempt, anyway.

"Have you notified the Beer Barons?"

Abel nods. "They're angry. They're not getting volume, but you're still cashing their checks."

The gang has pulled seventeen random, careful jobs in six months. With each heist, Trevino feels he's being laughed at.

"Put together a team. A dozen men. Make them mean. Lethal. I want this gang ended."

The Water Czar enters the press room, stands tall behind his podium. "The UWA is assembling a special task force to identify and apprehend the Hole In The Well Gang." Trevino wishes he knew who named them. You don't name criminals for the same reason you don't name livestock you plan to eat: it engenders mercy.

~o~

Six months before, Henry Hill was planting rice with his Ma and his brothers down south, or at least trying to. They were long past 'barely enough to get by.'

Henry discovered the UWA Explorer Program: volunteers needed for one-year commitments. Using old oil company drilling logs, their plan was to find the best places to pump brackish water from the state's aquifers, trillions of gallons

26

in the subsurface to be treated and made usable: find the well sites, build the plants, break the drought's back. The Inland Desalination Plant bill was stalled in Austin for a fourth straight year, but UWA wanted to be ready. It was a paying job: room, board, and a water bonus. Henry figured it was one less mouth for Ma to feed, the water bonus would go home to her, and his brothers could handle the meager harvest.

Henry was two years too young to apply. He skirted that by creating Walter Kidd. The fake ID was easy. Fudged stats made Kidd two inches taller and turned hazel eyes blue. A scruffy beard and moustache, once grown, complimented Henry's bushy hair. The altered picture resembled Henry Hill, but less-so if you studied it too long: straighter jaw, sharper cheekbones, thinner lips. A random Walter Kidd in the Social Security Death Index supplied the social security number.

The Kid was assigned to West Division Team 14, Baker's Team. He joined them on the road outside Brownwood. The day he arrived, Baker informed The Kid everything he'd been told was a lie. "I stumbled on it a month ago. Trevino has a secret operation that's already pumping brackish water from test wells and selling it off the books."

"Black market water?"

"Yes. Corporate customers process it, then sell beer or soda or more expensive water to the public. They get rich while people go thirsty. I can't prove it yet. But I aim to disrupt the works until I can."

Baker gave The Kid the option to stick or go home. The Kid joined the gang. Why not? If Baker was right, The Kid didn't mind squeezing Trevino for every tear Ma cried while running a farm on rations and rain dances. What better cover than working for the man you wanted to bedevil?

~o~

It's a new day.

WDT-14 spends it perched over a seventy-year-old well cut by the long-busted West Catskill Oil Company. Drill, tap, test. Brackish water confirmed at 748 feet. Baker reports it to the UWA and confirms their next stop.

That night, a driver named Richter sees a dead horse lying in the middle of the road in the headlights. He's heard stories. Decides not to stop. The horse is painted sandbags filled with spikes. On flat tires, Richter loses 7,500 gallons to the Hole In The Well Gang.

~o~

The Kid rides in the drill rig cab with Baker and Drake. Reads online news while he filters his cut of water from the tanker job through shell companies, on its way to Ma. He might be the first person to commit water laundering. "Says here Trevino is sending a hand-picked team of deputies after us. He calls us deplorable."

Drake snorts. "I'd rather be despicable."

"He's annoyed," Baker says. "Time to step things up."

The gang plumbs five more tankers over two weeks. Makes it rain for fifteen more farms.

They raid a warehouse outside San Marcos, liberate five pallets of bottled water, and distribute it to three poor schools along their route.

They sabotage one of Trevino's pumping operations. Baker figures his team drilled the well, it's his to break. The Kid snatches a laptop from the foreman's trailer. He knows what the right computer can tell them. This one sits inside a locked cage–looks right enough. Once it's noticed missing, it'll become a fancy paperweight, so The Kid hacks through the night.

Turns out the computer is the fullest reservoir in Texas.

The Kid is exhausted when the gang rises. "A network guy was upgrading the pump site. His laptop had everything

I needed to log into the UWA mainframe. I cracked Trevino's official email account."

Baker's eyes grow saucer-big. "Tell me you found something."

"Nah. It's so clean, it squeaks when he logs in. But his secret account, WATERCZAR1? He should have hid that a little better."

For someone surrounded by water, Trevino's hands are dirt-brown. The emails confirm sales of unprocessed water to corporations. Kickbacks for off-book allotment. Fees on contracts to import bottled water from the north, plus a cut of the mark-up. Substitutions of treated stadium wastewater for fresh groundwater. Back-dated drill permits to circumvent the private well moratorium. Skimmed Federal Disaster Relief funds. It goes on and on, hundreds of exchanges between Trevino and a web of people swapping hard cash for liquid favors.

Drake reads exchanges between the three legislators Trevino's paying to block the Inland Desalination Plant bill. "He's timing the deal so he can use it to run for governor."

Baker never smiles. He smiles now.

The Kid clones it all and burns it to a disc. The gang buys The Kid breakfast, a steak so big he can't finish it.

~o~

Abel pokes his head into Trevino's office. "The Hole In The Well Gang finally stepped in it."

Trevino's left eye jumps. It's begun twitching every time someone mentions the gang. "Explain."

"They took a laptop in a pump station raid last night. It's equipped with anti-theft tracking. We're triangulating their location now."

Trevino's eye stops twitching. He grins, a crocodile. "Send my boys when you're ready."

Trevino's Boys. Picked by Abel, fully deputized by the state police at Trevino's request, their numbers include:

Kane Powers. Former Texas pistol trick-shot champion. Hasn't missed a target ten years running, including the Hispanic kid he caught taking a drink from his garden hose. Acquitted.

Rudy Martinez. Ex-Special Forces recon. His sergeant says Martinez can track a flea in a sandstorm. His discharge papers recommend long-term psychological care.

And Chuck. Just Chuck. Quiet until he isn't. Then he's all kinds of noise. Best met in libraries or churches, though both frown on his Ruger Mini-14.

The others are a stew of skilled marksmen and vicious misanthropes. Once the gang is dialed in, Abel opens the chute and Trevino's Boys ride.

~o~

The Kid jumps at the gunshot and the crash of shattered glass in the darkness behind him. He lays flat in the scrub grass. More shots punch the sides of both tankers. The gang's pump whines and dies.

Baker and Ramirez duck behind the pick-up. Marco scrambles under the vehicle. Drake doesn't make it, perforated by a dozen bullets. His body jerks and falls. His shotgun clatters away.

The Kid hears footfalls behind him. They stop on the road, six feet to his left.

"Wait for it." A whisper, not to The Kid.

The gang's tanker detonates. Night becomes day. Covered by the noise, The Kid rolls onto his back. Sees two men with big guns. Distracted by their clean line of sight to Baker, they overlook The Kid right beside them.

At the right range, even a bean bag gun can be lethal.

The Kid's first round strikes a tattooed man in the Adam's

apple, breaking his neck. Kane Powers sees The Kid in time to catch the second shot between the eyes. He takes another round in the chest. Skull fracture, broken ribs, and internal bleeding add up fast. Powers falls and never rises.

Baker and Ramirez lay down cover for Marco. He slips behind the wheel, starts the pick-up. Climbing into the bed, Ramirez takes a bullet in the shoulder.

Marco drives at The Kid, never hesitates. Baker stands on the running board, one arm around the side of the truck. He grabs The Kid's arm as they pass. The Kid jumps aboard.

It's a mile before The Kid can maneuver into the cab from the bed. He throws the laptop out the broken passenger window. He never thought to check for an anti-theft device. He feels like the architect of the ambush.

They debate returning for Drake's body, decide against suicide. They double-back on their route three times before returning to the farm. They stash the pickup in the barn and wait. No one comes for them.

~o~

They'd lick their wounds if they had spit.

The Kid explains how they were found. Marco stitches up Ramirez. Baker tells them, "Drake's body in UWA's hands means they'll know who we are by sun-up. We need to run."

Ramirez stands watch outside. Marco packs supplies. Baker takes The Kid into the next room. Hands The Kid an envelope with cash inside. A lot of cash.

"What's this?"

"Severance. Anyone asks, I'll tell 'em you died on the job and I've been pocketing your pay and drinking your water."

"But... I'm with you guys."

Baker shakes his head. "Not any more."

"If this is about them finding us–"

"It's not."

"Then the two guys I shot—"

"The guys you shot are on all of us."

"Then *why*?"

"So you can live, Kid. We all signed on with UWA under our real names. We have to run. You forged your way in. Even if they look for you, they'll be chasing a ghost in Waco."

The Kid says nothing. Looks at the cash.

"You can get out. Lay low for a couple days, then go home to your Ma. Buy a desalinator. Drill her a well. Grow rice. Make it rain for you and yours." Baker hands him the notebook and disk. "Take this. I figure Trevino will try to bury us in unmarked graves. If he does, I want you to plant our cross in his chest."

The Kid takes the notebook and disk, nods. He doesn't cry, though it hurts to be turned out. He doesn't rage, doesn't argue. Just nods. A promise.

He fills his canteen. Tucks away his severance and Baker's notebook. Shaves off the beard and the moustache and trims his hair to a crew-cut. Burns Walter Kidd's ID and retrieves his own, sewn into his jacket for safekeeping.

Henry Hill leaves the farm on foot a couple hours before dawn. He walks four miles into town and waits for a used car dealer along the highway to open. He buys a beat-up Chevy Nova for $1,000 cash. Gases up and drives to the next town. Holes up in a motel.

~o~

Once Trevino learns WDT-14 is the Hole In The Well Gang, he plasters their pictures everywhere: news, web, social media. A water reward is offered. Tips flood in. A motorist spots the gang's pick-up at a highway rest stop. Trevino's Boys catch up with them on I-10, an hour shy of Houston. Ten men versus three, semi-automatic rifles versus shotguns and pistols on a wide, flat stretch of asphalt. It's over before the state police arrive.

A mile of the interstate is closed for six hours to clean up the mess.

Henry watches it unfold on CNN over cold cereal in his motel room. Initially, there's talk of Walter Kidd, suspected fifth member, still at large. Henry's manufactured picture of Kidd looks like a stranger on TV. An hour later, they report Walter Kidd's social security number belongs to a man who died thirty years ago. No one knows what's real.

Trevino lies from his podium with cool expertise. "The members of the Hole In The Well Gang were unemployed oilfield workers. Drifters. We believe they murdered and assumed the identities of a UWA drill team. This gave them intimate knowledge of our operations, and allowed them to commit their crimes while hiding in plain sight."

Henry puts on gloves and writes what he knows about each member of the gang at the end of the notebook. He tucks the last of the gang's calling cards between the pages. Seals the notebook and disk in an envelope, wiping everything down as he goes.

Henry checks out and points the Nova towards Austin.

~o~

Security cameras don't capture the face of the man who leaves the package with the Austin Republic receptionist. It's marked CONFIDENTIAL FOR KITTY ANDERSON. Anderson writes features. She will never manage Trevino's fan club, though she might dance on his grave. She unwraps the package and reads the card, then the notebook, then the emails.

It's one long kiss in the rain.

~o~

Henry drives. Faces and deeds taunt his thoughts, what

he's done and what was done for him. He wonders if anyone will still be looking for The Kid once the fire starts under Trevino. He'd rather The Kid become a campfire story.

Clouds darken as he travels south. He hears a clap of thunder, then another. He pulls over and gets out, anticipating rain. It would be nice, Henry thinks, to at least feel clean before he sees Ma again.

The sky threatens, then lightens. The front passes, Mother Nature as the world's greatest burlesque queen.

—o—

DIAL "C"
FOR CONSULTANT

TWO GOONS. IT'S ALMOST always two goons.
Sometimes three, if their boss is insecure. This time? Two.

You can tell by the dull eyes that henchmen aren't full
of information. That makes them both safe and expendable.
These two were told what they needed to know, and nothing
more: where to pick me up, what I looked like, the route to
travel to mask their ultimate destination–as if I couldn't figure
that out anyway.

They scanned me to ensure I wasn't carrying weapons or
tracking devices. Then the one with dirty blonde surfer hair
that came out of a bottle handed me the hood. I pulled it on.
Day became night in the back of the limo. At least this one
sent a limo. The ones that send vans never seem as serious
about their plans for world domination.

Surfer Hair knocked on the glass to tell the driver to go.
As a rule, the blindfolded trip to any lair took at least an hour,

as long as ninety minutes with doubling back. We'd gone a mile when Surfer Hair wanted to make small talk.

"So, you're really him?"

"Yes, " I said, "I'm really him."

"Huh. You don't look like him."

Some days, just getting to the gig wasn't worth my fee. "No? And you're an expert?"

"My old man had the magazines." Surfer Hair sounded underwhelmed. "Most of my friends' dads had stashes of Playboy or Hustler. Mine? Superhero crap. I think he was a member of your fan club or something. I couldn't give that stuff away when he died."

There had been an Iron Vanguard fan club, but that had dried up years before. How many members were there at its peak? Fifty thousand? I couldn't remember. It was hard enough remembering the names of everyone on the nemesis and arch-nemesis lists. "That was eighty pounds of muscle and a heart bypass ago, kid."

"I didn't think you guys got old."

Everyone gets old, genius, I thought. *It just feels worse when strength and agility are your bread and butter.* I said instead, "Unless we heal or can manipulate time, I assure you: we do."

The ears were still sharp. I heard his face crease when his gaze narrowed in suspicion. "How does the boss even know he can trust a 'good guy'?"

"Kid, I couldn't punch my way out of a wet paper bag these days. I've got a hitch in my left hip where a missile hit me. It groans when it's going to rain. I had a cataract taken off my right eye two years ago. And not that it's any of your business, but I need to get up at least twice a night to piss. The only way I can still make it in this world is to tell men like your boss where their operations are vulnerable, in exchange for large sacks of money." I paused. Timing was a superpower all its own. "Don't make me start by telling him he needs a higher grade of henchman."

That shut him up. Then I got to ride in peace.

~o~

I hadn't been the Iron Vanguard for fifteen years, but I'd known my run was coming to an end a few years before I hung up the suit. It's a lot like being a ball player. You start fresh, with that 'save the world' fire in your belly. You win a lot, have a bunch of good seasons, rack up some impressive stats, get your face on trading cards. Maybe you do a responsible endorsement or two.

Then you pull a muscle that's never been trouble before, or you get beat up and it hurts a few extra days. You realize you're not the rookie anymore. But you hang in there, you play through the pain, and you still believe you can change the course of human events with a single swing. It's a hope you cling to until the day you get knocked out of the game by something that wouldn't have fazed you in your prime.

For me, that was an old Trailways bus in Egg Harbor Township, New Jersey. The guy who threw it at me called himself the Mechanical Wonder. Jeez, he could throw. That bus hit me like a pile-driver. I lost my wind, then lost consciousness. I was down for ninety-seven seconds before some local woke me up. I was still able to finish; there's a reason they ask, "Whatever became of the Mechanical Wonder?" in Egg Harbor. It didn't make the news, my brief, inglorious blackout, but those ninety-seven seconds made me realize the Iron Vanguard's day had passed.

And like that, the life of a superhero changes forever. Except there's no medical, dental or pension plans for guys like me, no parade when you hang up the suit. Do you know who gives you cake when you retire from saving the world? If you live in Florida, it's the lady behind the bakery counter at the Publix Supermarket.

~o~

My client was beside the limousine when Surfer Hair removed my hood and ushered me from the vehicle. We were in a small auto garage, four spots with trucks, twelve more with jeeps. The jeeps were old, military surplus, tricked out with machine guns. If the public knew how many wannabe super-villains bought their arms at government surplus sales, they'd go blind with rage. The lines on the concrete were bright with fresh yellow paint. Old construction, recent renovation.

I hadn't met my client in person before that moment. He'd contacted me through my website, Dial "C" for Consultant. It still amazes me I'm not into that one comic book publisher a few bucks for the riff.

I was old enough to be my client's father, but the gap in our ages wasn't much wider than that. His eyes were stony blue and serious. The tip of his nose was hooked. He'd gone with the shaved head look, but didn't wear it well. His goatee was the wrong shape for his chin. The jagged scar that ran from below his right ear to his jaw line was livid pink, fresh enough to suggest a motivation for his new-found villainy.

He wore a well-tailored gray suit that said he yearned for respect–not as expensive as the ones Crimson Deathmonger used to wear, or as fancy as BlankSlate's, though BlankSlate had always been more flash than bang anyway. He offered his hand and I shook it. On a ten-scale, his grip was a seven.

"Mister Cronin," he said. "I'm Professor Entropy."

"It's good to finally meet you."

"Do you prefer Mister Cronin, or should I call you Iron Vangu–"

"Cronin is fine, Professor," I interrupted. "I find there are often employees within my clients' enterprises that get nervous when they hear what I used to do." I shot an obvious glance at Surfer Hair. Professor Entropy scowled at his minion. Mission accomplished.

38

We walked to the elevators. "I've had my chef prepare lunch," Entropy said. "I find it helpful to fortify before touring the entire facility. The place covers a lot of ground, and one of the trams is down for repair."

I didn't have the heart to tell him my digestive tract had become finicky, and that his lunch was probably going to make my guts churn. Sometimes, being a hero is being a gracious guest.

~o~

Over lunch, a series of dim sum dishes that I have to admit were exquisite in preparation, he asked The Question.

I hadn't had a single client in nine years of consulting that hadn't asked The Question. Some couched it in careful words and tones. Others were direct to the point of insult. I didn't blame them. I'd have asked the same thing if our roles were reversed. On the bell curve of The Question, Entropy fell on the slope towards the direct side.

"How does someone with a sterling background as a hero," he asked, "come to consult with people in the profession of world domination? You probably stopped or eliminated some forty criminal masterminds in your day. I would suspect there's a huge conflict of interest, if not heart."

"It was fifty-three criminal masterminds," I corrected. "Fifty-five if you count the three versions of the Clonemeister as individuals." I wiped my chin with no regrets over enjoying the shrimp shumai. "It didn't happen overnight. My record on the side of the law speaks for itself, and I don't pretend to hide it. But in many ways, I'm like a soldier in an unpopular war."

Entropy cocked his head. "I don't follow."

"The people I served loved me when I could turn a city-destroying giant robot into scrap metal, or fight my way into a place like this and bring out a criminal in irons." I sighed. "But then my powers began to falter. I couldn't move as quickly, or hit with the same impact. Other players emerged. I wound up on the sidelines, then had to put myself out to pasture. In short, Professor, I got old." I took a sip of plum wine and saw Entropy nodding. "The only thing I've ever been good at was being a superhero. Do you know what that pays? Adoration until you retire, and then maybe they call you to judge a talent show or sit on a float in a parade. They see you as a set of powers. They believe when your arm noodles, you've lost your value."

Entropy's manservant rolled the dim sum cart to the table for the tenth time. The man's face was neutral. I couldn't tell if he was bored or mortified to be playing waiter. I felt bad for him. I signaled my satisfaction, and Entropy waved him away. "But you had tremendous institutional knowledge and experience."

"I did. I busted into or destroyed more criminal strongholds than most of my contemporaries. The authorities didn't care. They thought of me as a broken toy: replace it with a new one that has louder noises and more accessories." I leaned forward and smiled. "That's when I realized the perfect market for my experience: men like you."

Entropy took his napkin from his lap and set it on the table. "What about justice?"

"I can't eat justice, Professor. When my left shoulder pops out of its socket because the Bangalore Menace dislocated it thirty years ago, justice doesn't pay for my emergency room visit. If my Ford dumps its transmission, justice won't even call me a tow truck. I know one thing: the business of stopping super-villains and evil geniuses. If they're going to pay me in untraceable bills to tell them how to reinforce their infrastructure against men and women like me?" I reached for my briefcase and the forms he needed to sign. "I have to look out for number one."

He seemed satisfied by my answer to The Question. I'd say one in twenty retained enough skepticism to thank me politely and drive me home. Could you blame them?

We adjourned to his office to take care of formalities.

~o~

Part of my ability to serve Professor Entropy's market was the contract into which my clients and I entered. On their part, they gave me all-area access to the facility, along with any construction particulars that were critical to analysis. You'd be amazed how many people have underwater lairs and don't think the crushing weight of water could be an issue. In addition, they agreed to protect my anonymity as a consultant, on pain of a penalty fee with an absurd number of zeros.

On my part, I agreed to not disclose any projects I witnessed in progress at the facility, including any planning I might become privy to in the course of my inspection, nor any details of the facility or its location to any federal, state or local law enforcement official. I agreed to provide a written analysis of the deficiencies discussed on our tour of the facility. I agreed to not take any photographs, film or audio recordings, or other media records of what I saw.

There were lots of small sub-clauses and legal mumbo-jumbo, boilerplate from a program I'd downloaded via the Internet. I could have had Blue Barrister put it together–we went back a few decades–but the fewer people that knew my business, the better. Also, Blue Barrister was a ball-buster.

Once the ink was dry and the wire-transfer of my fee to my account in Bern was confirmed, I pulled out my clipboard of forms and my pencil. Professor Entropy ushered me into a small elevator adjacent to his office. "Most of the lifts serve specific floor groups," he said, and thumbed the lowest button on the control board. "This one can access any level in the facility."

"Is it cable drive, or does it use alternative methods?"

"It's conventional. I think."

I made my first notes. "Right off the bat, you'll want to install charges to sever the cable, and steel plates that can be closed across the shaft at multiple points in an emergency. Nothing dares a hero to take your place down more than an unguarded central access point."

Entropy looked like I'd sucker-punched him. I didn't need powers to detect the nascent pout on the man's lips.

~o~

Four hours. Down and up, side to side. By the time we were done, I'd sharpened my pencil a half-dozen times and my feet felt like they had burst into flame.

Entropy had gotten a great deal on a natural cavern. It wasn't the most spacious place, but the infrastructure was already 90% complete. He told me survivalists had sold it to him, but the build-out spoke to more money than you found in the end-of-the-world set. I suspect a different villain had gone bust on facilities before getting around to things like doomsday weapons and killer androids.

We fell into a pattern that was familiar. All evil geniuses are certain they've created an environment that will survive a full-frontal assault by armies, supers, atomic bombs or the Rapture. They fall in love with their own ideas because they're the boss, often for the first time. The need to assert control over every detail overrides things like common sense.

Entropy was a victim of the same self-deluding pride. He would bring me into an area for inspection. A doting father with a 500 watt grin, he'd explain the beautiful features and genius of his young child. Then I'd point out how the child had soiled itself, burped up lunch, or set fire to the rug.

"But if you put the armory here, Professor, your men will need to pass through Medical to get weapons and ammunition. With the first strike, your enemy creates casualties that make a choke point from which you'll never recover.

"You may be trying to shield the server room from an EMP, but given the cave was formed by running water, having the servers so close to the bottom invites someone to flood your hardware as their opening gambit.

"Are those storage racks anti-static and vibration-dampening? Do you want the ordinance going off without being fired? Do you know the size of the fireball you're begging for?

"Well, yes–an alligator pit *does* make a statement. But how often do you expect to bring your enemies here just to kill them? That's wasted space and a lot of alligator care and feeding in the meantime. Not cheap, Professor.

"Propane tanks?!? For the love of–Professor, no one in their right mind is storing hydrocarbons five stories below the ground in a location with a target painted on it!"

He'd paid six figures for an honest assessment. I wasn't going to sugar coat it.

Entropy took it all with a stiff upper lip, but by the time we were done I could tell he was tired of listening to my observations. He absented himself while I reviewed the structural data pertinent to the facility. From the cigarette stink on him when he returned, I suspected he'd gone topside for a smoke and to call me names.

~o~

Entropy hefted my final analysis. It came in at twenty-six pages, most of it form-based. His facility wasn't in dire shape. I'd toured one in Toledo once that would have gone up in flames if you'd looked at it cross-eyed. But Entropy's place did need work. He opened to a random page, frowned. "Wow. Are all these things really necessary?"

"Only if you don't want your run at global domination ended before you can make your first serious ransom demand."

He thumbed through it. I doubted he would ever read the

whole thing. "You wouldn't have anyone you work with to correct the items you find?"

I snapped my briefcase closed. "You mean like a contractor?"

"Yes. Like that."

"I don't recommend specific vendors, for the sake of the anonymity of everyone concerned. I'm sure you understand."

"Oh. Of course, yes."

We parted with a handshake in his topside vehicle depot. Then I was bundled into the limousine once more, this time by two different goons, and driven back to the city, hood in place. No one spoke to me. Surfer Hair had probably told them not to. I cat-napped. I wished there'd been someone to rub my feet.

~o~

It was after six when I sat down with Marty Bolan for dinner. Marty and I go all the way back to college. He was a reporter who'd made his big-time bones interviewing the Iron Vanguard at the start of the superhero's career. It's a thin line between friendship and nepotism. These days, he's a managing features editor with FedNews Monthly. Dinner is usually on him.

"Anything interesting going on?" he asked.

"I went spelunking today."

"Yeah? Where?"

"A cavern outside of the city." I sipped my water. "It was interesting, but I probably won't go back."

"Why not?"

"The whole place is unstable. From the geologic survey I saw, a couple of strong tremblers would bring the whole place down."

"Sounds dangerous."

I scribbled two sets of coordinates on a napkin and pushed

it across the table. "Yeah. ManQuake the Earth-shaker should never–and I mean never–be allowed anywhere near these two locations. It would devastate a fantastic dim sum place I just discovered."

Marty stared at me, a thin smile on his lips. "Uh-huh. Excuse me a minute." He took the napkin and excused himself to make a call.

I know what you're thinking: that I'm a horrible person to mislead people who hire me to make their businesses safer, that I should get all the way out of the game if I'm not going to play fair. But it's like I told Professor Entropy, as I've told the others I've helped take down in my new life as a consultant: being a hero is the only thing I know how to do, whether I bend steel with my bare hands, or struggle to cut a sandwich. And a guy still has to live. Even as an informant, this life doesn't pay.

A smart villain would shoot me in the head when I'm done giving him an assessment, just to remove any lingering doubts. To walk into a place knowing that could happen, and that I couldn't stop it if it did? I would argue that takes nerves of steel.

The rest of it?

That's just salesmanship.

–o–

THE JAIL IN SHINJUKU WARD

CONSCIOUSNESS BROUGHT PAIN AND Richard swooned. He felt medicated. His flesh burned as if seared on a grill. His lips throbbed, and he fought to open his stinging eyes.

Stone walls surrounded him, soot-dark. The floor was dry, cracked earth. Small flames neither dispensed warmth nor dispelled shadows. Shackles hugged his wrists and ankles, pinched his skin. He felt a draft and realized he was naked.

He groaned. A cry that begged pity creaked in answer from the dark.

How had Richard gotten here? He'd been cutting across the 5 Chrome Ginza to catch up with the university tour group at the train for Kyoto. He remembered an alley leading away from the neon lights, the stench of animal offal, greasy puddles. He remembered a strangled cry. Was it his own voice? It seemed like days ago.

From the darkness, a moan coalesced into a word Richard

didn't know. "Yurei!"

Figures glided into the torch light. Richard saw elegant blue silk robes festooned with unknown sutras. Cold eyes studied him. The five, all Japanese, spoke native tongue among themselves before one stepped forward, the leader. His English was studied, if not polished. "Dark Kagiia must be kept. The place is prepared."

They pulled the husk of the moaning old man into the light. His sunken eyes stared without aim. His skin showed the colors of purification. Richard saw the man's face was covered to the eyelids in uneven columns of hiragana and katakana writing, but there was something wrong with the characters. Richard tried to conjure a memory, a lecture or reading about Japanese script. It eluded him.

Richard watched the robed figures pierce the old man with a curved blade. They bled him into a clay bowl. He sighed in death, and his husk was laid aside.

Richard was powerless when the men then raised the bowl to his lips. Blood washed over his swollen tongue and down his throat, hot and sour. They followed it with brackish water. Richard's head buzzed. He was certain they'd poisoned him.

Shackles were unlocked. Richard slid down the wall, crumpled in a pile. He wanted to vomit, but couldn't. "Why are you doing this?"

"Dark Kagiia is secure," the leader said. "Life continues."

The robed men tried to assist Richard. He swung a rubbery arm, noticed the shadow on his skin. He stilled, studied himself in the flickering half-light. Feet, legs, groin, stomach, arms– his entire body was dark with lines of Japanese characters, the same unusual columns of writing as on the old man. The source of the pain in his eyes and lips became clear.

Inside his head, the buzz became a lament, a threat, a bellow. As it grew louder within his skull, Richard studied his hands. His scream mingled with Dark Kagiia's.

Not poison. They'd done something worse: the writing. A spell to keep evil out, inscribed in his flesh.

In reverse.

—o—

LOREM IPSUM DONALD

Waiting for the left turn from M Street onto the Key Bridge, Donald absently pulled on his left ear and it came off in his fingertips with a wine cork 'pop.'

For a moment, what happened didn't register, his mind on traffic and being on time for his meeting in Crystal City. He looked down at the curve of pink skin in his hand, familiar and still alien from its new perspective. Awareness struck with the force of the truck in the next lane making a sudden pivot, and Donald dropped the curl of skin in his lap. It tumbled to the floor by his feet.

"Nonononono." His fingers probed the side of his head where the ear had been. The tip of his index finger found a hole and traced it with caution. He pulled it away expecting blood and gore, cancerous black tissue, some other sign of pending death. But his finger was as clean as when he'd started.

Behind him, a driver leaned on the horn. Donald noticed despite missing an ear, he still heard in full stereo.

He fought down a dizzy wave of panic and turned through the light. On the other side of the bridge, he whipped the car into a hotel parking lot and stopped across three spaces.

He felt around the floor mat for the ear. It was most of the way under the seat. He retrieved it with cautious fingers. Dirt and stray hair stuck to it. He turned it in his hand. It felt like his ear. If the front was flesh, the back had a smooth, hard peg as big around as a Ticonderoga No. 2 pencil. A canal ran through it. The outside of the peg was crusted with what looked like dried glue, waxy yellow.

Donald thought about brushing the ear clean. He instead set it on the passenger seat. He angled the visor mirror to examine the side of his head. There was a matching hole in which the peg had once set. *Like Mister Potato Head*, he thought. He considered trying to reattach it, left it instead on the seat beside him. He was afraid to break it or somehow ruin the hole in his head by forcing it.

An emergency room? Losing an ear probably qualified, but who on earth specialized in snap-on parts? Donald considered his fate as a specimen in a glass room, maniacs with wild eyes taking bets on what else would pop off, given the opportunity and a little help.

He wasn't bleeding. He could hear. His little voice urged him to go home first, before signing up as a medical sideshow. He could think at home. Colleen would help him sort it out.

~o~

Donald arrived home to unexpected silence.

Colleen didn't work. His job with the firm took care of them both. His wife's typical day involved garden projects and keeping the house. Dinner was ready most nights when Donald got home. Grocery day was Tuesday. Thursday afternoons, she went out with girlfriends. Her car was in the garage, but the house was dark, graveside quiet.

The last week or so, something had been on her mind. Warm and talkative by nature, Colleen had turned turtle on him. His direct question about it elicited only a faint smile. "I'm just tired," she told him. It felt like a deflection. Had he hurt her somehow? Disappointed her? He'd been on a project that was making his days longer, but the problem driving that was drawing to a close. Was she sick? Restless? She was disinclined to offer him clues.

He heard a small sound, a scraping somewhere deeper in the house. If anything, the hole without an ear was stronger, more attuned. He followed the sound up the stairs and down the hall to the master suite.

The bedroom door was half open. Donald pushed it the rest of the way. It swung wide on silent hinges. Colleen was making the scraping sound, a consequence of her body's movements rubbing the headboard of their bed against the wall. The man on top of her was helping: he was rocking Colleen.

Donald stood in the doorway, a visitor in an oddly familiar red-light district. He couldn't find his voice. He'd never had cause to question Colleen's fidelity; yet here she was, having sex with a stranger in their bed. It stung Donald more that it appeared to be good sex, based on Colleen's response. He studied Colleen's body; not a runner's form anymore–she'd abandoned that when her knees began to bother her–but still very fit. He loved her curves, the lines of her legs, how they flowed from her hips. Were the tableau not emasculating, he might have gotten aroused.

Was this her distraction? Was he one of those husbands so involved in work he'd neglected her to the point of her seeking someone else to meet her needs? And who the hell was he? For a moment, Donald had forgotten he was missing an ear. Now he contemplated taking a replacement off someone else.

He wasn't sure how long he'd been there when Colleen, closer to orgasm than Donald had ever managed to take her, noticed him. Eros vanished in the width of a scream.

Donald stepped into the hall. Behind him, he heard Colleen scramble from the bed and stalk around the room. She emerged, pulling the bedroom door closed behind her. Her bathrobe was still loose. Little glimpses of pale skin appeared and vanished, whitecaps in a blue cotton sea. Her cheeks were still flushed. "What are you doing home?"

"I'm your husband and I live here. Though it looks like you've got half of that covered."

He tried to read her expression, but it confused him. Despite the rosy glow that was either sex or embarrassment, there was a calm in her eyes. She'd been caught in the act and wasn't sorry.

"Why aren't you at work?" She gathered her robe and sashed it closed, ignoring the elephant behind the bedroom door. "Don't you have a meeting at one?"

"You're having sex with a stranger in our bed in the middle of the day, and you think I need a meeting reminder?" She stared at him. "How long has this has been going on?"

"Look, this is awkward for all of us—"

"Throwing up at Christmas dinner is awkward. This is a level beyond." He took a step towards the bedroom. Colleen blocked his way.

"Why are you here?" Her head tipped as she looked at him, the way a person notices a change but fails to see the haircut. "Something's off."

"Interesting choice of words." He reached into his shirt pocket and handed her the ear.

Colleen held it up in the low light. Turned it in her hand, pinched it between her fingers. She shook her head and tossed the ear aside. It bounced once on the carpet and came to rest at an angle against the wall. The baseboard look like an eavesdropper.

"You doodled with it, didn't you? Like a kid with a loose tooth." Her voice was a stew of anxiety and wonder and,

Donald thought, relief.

He retrieved the appendage. "I'm sick, Colleen. Something's wrong with me. I need your help."

The bedroom door opened. Donald looked past Colleen at himself.

No. Not himself. Not quite.

Donald might have been looking at an airbrushed photo of himself. The stranger had his features: the cast and color of the eyes, the thin slope of nose, the shape of the lips. But the line of his jaw was firmer. His cheekbones were higher. His face had a smoother shape, his head more hair. He was four inches taller. Shirtless, his torso displayed muscles of which Donald had heard, but never taken the time to develop.

Donald turned from the reflection of himself to Colleen. "Who the hell is this?"

"Colleen." Donald wasn't sure if the stranger had his voice. The man beckoned Colleen towards the bedroom.

She passed him, glanced over his shoulder at Donald. "I'm sorry." She whispered in the stranger's ear. The stranger kissed her cheek and came into the hallway, closing the door behind him.

"Let's go downstairs and talk," he said. "You don't have much time."

~o~

In the kitchen, the stranger–*the Donaldgänger*, Donald thought–tried to explain, but it was gibberish. "You're winding down."

"People don't wind down. They aren't grandfather clocks. They get sick. They die."

"True. People don't. But you're not a person. You're a placeholder."

Donald turned his ear in his hands. Its color was fading. Bits of the skin flecked off and fell to the table like snowflakes.

"I don't believe you."

"She had you created." The Donaldgänger was calm. From his manner, Donald wondered if he was a doctor, a counselor of some kind.

"That's impossible. I remember my entire life. I grew up in the Hudson Valley in New York. My father drove a truck. I went to school in Chicago. Colleen and I met–"

"–at a party your friend Monica threw, seven years ago," the Donaldgänger picked up the thread. "You got married two years later. You told your best man, Wally, you were scared to death. It's all implants." He paused. Donald could see the man was parsing his words. "Colleen selected basic attributes and phenotypes and personality traits. Those were imprinted on a 36-month organic template. Instant history. You were 'born'"–he emphasized with finger quotes Donald found offensive–"fully formed, with a lifetime of memories."

"This kind of thing isn't possible. They can barely clone sheep."

"No? You resent your father for missing your little league games. Your first sexual experience was at fifteen with Dotty Cowling's cousin Barbara, in Dotty's garage. You once stole $40 for pot from your roommate's girlfriend, but the pot made you sick. Only time you ever tried it. Ever tell anyone any of these things?"

Donald shook his head, stared. "If I'm some placeholder, what the hell are you?"

"I'm the final draft. A genetically engineered rapid build from an egg and donor DNA. I represent Colleen's revisions, the lessons learned in making her ideal man."

Donald made fists of his shaking hands. "I'm supposed to accept this? Sit back and let you have my life?"

"You weren't supposed to come back today. Prototypes are designed to seek a quiet place to wind down. You've proven more sturdy than expected."

Donald's head swam. He wondered if something else was

56

about to fall off. "Who's responsible for all this?"

The Donaldgänger took a banana from the basket on the table, peeled it, spoke between bites. "They're called The Noble Corporation. You'll never find them. They prefer to remain anonymous."

"You can take me to them."

"I don't know where they are. I have our implanted memories, plus the background information they program in the event this happens. But I woke up on a Metro train this morning, between stops. In a couple of hours, I'll forget the programming details, this conversation, you. I'll be Donald Farris. You'll be gone."

"I'm going to find them, this Noble Corporation. And when they explain how to undo this, I'm coming back. You'd better not be here when I do. This is my life."

"*Was* your life. That's over." The reflection tossed the banana peel in the garbage. "I'm Donald Farris. Who's going to doubt that?"

Donald rose. His move towards the cutlery block was stopped by the stranger's grip on his arm. Donald struggled, but felt a looseness in his left shoulder. The Donaldgänger felt it too and relented. He pushed Donald towards the door. Donald knew he was physically incapable of stopping the man.

"Leave," the stranger said. "There's nothing here for you anymore."

Donald glared. He walked through the door and crossed the small porch. Behind him, the Donaldgänger closed the door.

"This isn't over!" Donald shouted. "Stay right here." He stumbled off the bottom step and into the yard. He saw Colleen at an upstairs window, watching. He pointed at her. "You too, Colleen!" He screamed, wanting the neighbors to hear, to step into their yards, to witness. "I'll be back! This is my house! My life!"

He walked to his car. His shoulder betrayed him with the whispered buzz of a nylon zipper. Donald felt his left arm slip loose. He stared at it where it landed on the driveway. He picked it up, laid it on the back seat with care. He slid behind the wheel, started the car, and backed out.

~o~

The phone book had an address for the Noble Corporation in Clarendon. The number led to an automated phone tree that went in circles.

The office was behind a locked wooden door on the second floor atrium of a commercial development. Through the glass panel, Donald saw an abandoned office, a layer of dust on the empty desks. A tarnished brass plaque by the door proclaimed NOBLE.

Donald considered breaking the glass. Concern his remaining arm might detach and wind up laying inside, out of reach, stopped him.

He searched the Internet on his phone, but there was no information about the Noble Corporation: no web page, no other addresses, not even rumors about the claims the Donaldgänger had made.

Donald shouted his frustration in the emptiness. As he walked back to the car, he decided with a new, strange calm the only answer was to kill both the Donaldgänger and his wife.

~o~

The pawn shop proprietor was on the high side of fifty. He watched Donald study the row of glass display cases. "Lose it in the war?"

"Huh?"

"Your arm."

"Yeah, the war." He'd dropped a knitted cap from a street

vendor onto his head to distract from the missing ear, but it was impossible to disguise the absence of a limb. He stopped in front of a display, pointed to the gun in the back. It was sleek, dark, compact. "How much is the Glock?"

The clerk looked from the gun to Donald. The sensations in Donald's face were becoming hit and miss. He wondered about his expression. Did the clerk see an unhinged vet with an ax to grind against his Uncle Sam?

"Four-fifty. I'll need your ID and permit. Five day wait to pick it up."

Donald nodded. He turned attention to the locked cases where rifles and shotguns cozied together. He couldn't remember if you could buy a shotgun without a wait in Virginia. *Can you even work a shotgun? You've got one arm. Recoil will probably knock it off at the shoulder if you did manage a shot, if the force doesn't snap you in two.*

"Get out," the clerk said.

"What?"

"You're a man who wants something. Maybe to rob a liquor store, or a drug dealer, or to kill your wife or lover or boyfriend, whatever. Doesn't matter. But I've been robbed enough to know that look, and that look is trouble, so get out before I call a cop."

"You don't understand."

The clerk's hand darted under the counter. He came up with a nickel-plated pistol.

As he did, Donald's vision blurred. There was a crackle, the sound of ice straining to support weight. He felt an itch in the corner of his eye and blinked. The crackle became a snapping. Donald had sudden tunnel vision in his left eye. He felt something tumble from the lower orbit of his eye socket, over his cheek. Fragments tinkled on the countertop.

"Jesus." The clerk was suddenly unsure what to do with the revolver.

Donald tried to close the broken eye. The lid no longer

worked, caught on a shard. He concentrated on the good eye, seized on the clerk's confusion to grab at the clerk's gun. He got fingers around the barrel, the cylinder pressed into his palm.

The clerk's bravado drowned in a wave of fear. He struggled to pull the gun back. Donald's wrist snapped at the joint like a pool cue, sending the clerk stumbling backwards. The glass of the shotgun display cracked when the clerk hit it. He recovered his balance. "You should have left!"

He aimed the pistol and stopped, noticing the fingers of Donald's hand still clenched in a death-grip around the gun. The clerk's mouth opened in a small, silent 'o'. He pitched the pistol and hand aside.

Before the clerk could open one of the locked cases and extract a shotgun, Donald hurried into the street and tried to blend into the crowd. When the police cars with urgent sirens passed, Donald was four blocks from the store. There was no blood from the stump where his hand had snapped off. The edges of the skin resembled parchment paper.

~o~

It was almost five when Donald tried to get into his building. Security stopped him. He was a horror despite his suit, no longer recognizable to guards with whom he'd exchanged greetings for years. His facial muscles were failing, his cheeks sagging, his expression slack. His right eye had broken while Donald waited for a bus. He was forced to remove his flapping eyelids. They were tissue-paper, tore off without pain. Donald was left a perpetual view of the world through matched keyholes. If the guards were unsettled by the empty sockets, they disguised it well.

"Donald Farris is in his office," security told him.

Donald had no ID. He'd lost his wallet somewhere. He began to argue, but felt a looseness in his mouth that

60

frightened him. He left when one of the guards threatened to phone police.

Donald walked along the canal path that paralleled M Street. He didn't want to be seen. His right foot began to grind under his weight as he walked. He was almost to the Key Bridge again, where the first of his body's rebellions had occurred, when he felt a horrible disconnection below his abdomen. There was no physical pain, but the sensation of his manhood rattling around, held to him only by his clothing, was a psychological grenade.

Wiping the smirk off the face of the Donaldgänger was a hazy dream. He considered leaping from the bridge. But as he studied the span choked with early evening commuters, he was compelled to cross to the other side of the street and follow the sidewalk past the bridge and the gas station beside the Exorcist steps, past the entrance to Georgetown University, "HOYA SAXA" painted on the stones facing the road, towards the C&O canal tow path and beyond.

Donald walked down an overgrown trail, favoring the ankle that was still half-attached. The sun went down. Scattered clouds overhead wore the last blush of day. Ahead, obscured by trees, he could hear the Potomac running. He wasn't far from a section of the falls, but there were no landmarks to gauge his progress.

The compulsion to go farther abated and Donald stopped. He looked to his right and saw what was left of the woman.

She watched him. She wore a sun dress. Her shape was feminine, but her exposed flesh was peeling as if from a horrible sunburn. Her legs, disconnected and straight in front of her, were growing thinner with each cloud of dead skin the breeze carried away. Her arms were gone, her ears with them. Her jaw hung crooked, attached on the left side alone. One unbroken eye, a soothing blue in the twilight, surged forward as if planning to leap from the socket. Dark hair slipped from her head a few strands at a time.

The sight of her would have repulsed him yesterday. Today, he sat beside her. They both heard his lower back snap as he reached the ground, feet splayed to the sides.

The woman spoke with care, favoring her jaw. "Who are you?"

"Donald."

"Millie."

Between the trees, they watched the river flow.

"Pete said something went wrong," Millie said. "I was making dinner when she walked in. I was supposed to stop yesterday." She fought to keep from blinking. "He said I was too skinny. That was it. Kept saying he was sorry. That he'd have kept me instead if he could."

Donald heard something small rustling the underbrush near the water's edge. "Why did you come here?"

"Don't know. Something said to. Walking in I saw shoes. Clothes. Here and there. Guess they send us here to die."

"Elephant graveyard," Donald mumbled.

They listened to the night descending. The far-off sounds of life in Georgetown were a playground taunt.

"It's not fair," Millie said. "I had plans. Dreams. My dreams are supposed to be hers? I was going to –"

There was a tearing sound. Millie's jaw dropped to the ground, her tongue with it. She stopped. Words came out as inarticulate gibbering. She began to wail. Instead of tears, splinters of glass fell, the last of her ruptured eye.

With what strength he had left, Donald swayed his upper body to the right and slumped to the ground beside Millie. She did the same, leaning into his armless embrace. What was left of her body shook.

Donald laid his head against Millie's shoulder and waited for the end of their winding down, for the compassionate wind to carry them away, and realized he was shaking too.

—o—

ARK OF THE REVENANT

JAPHETH FIRED A TORCH for his father. "I was walking the deck above when I heard the griffin scream."

"Which of the other animals attacked it?" They were nine days into the voyage. Noah wasn't yet ready for the beasts to be killing each other.

"I do not know. I came for you as soon as I found it."

Japheth led Noah down the access ladders from the level where the family kept quarters to the deck second from the bottom. The lowest deck was ballast, supplies, and the dragon enclosure. The dragons were down there for everyone's protection. Above them, the next-largest animals were housed.

Their sandals scraped the wood of the deck, stray pieces of straw from the pens bending underfoot. The vast enclosure stunk of a hundred varieties of piss and shit. The voices of the animals enveloped them, a stew of murmurs from the shadows beyond reach of the torch's light.

One cry grew louder, separating from the others as Noah and his son drew closer. It was the cry of the female griffin. Noah didn't need illumination to recognize her mourning wail.

The male lay in the aisle outside their enclosure. The door was ripped open from the outside, the wood of the latch a mass of jagged splinters. The female stood beside him with wings upswept, as if in prayer. A long, low keen issued from deep within. Japheth stroked the large beast's coat as Noah crouched over her fallen companion.

The male griffin had died in violence. A torn wing and patches of mane littered the deck. Feathers mingled with the straw. Brilliant pools of scarlet blood filled the gouges left by his large claws in the deck. Savage bites marred his handsome face and broad throat.

"This is deviltry," Noah whispered. The cry of the female knifed his heart. He stood and turned to Japheth. "There are only so many beasts aboard with the ability to do this. We must find and secure it. Wake your brothers. Bring additional torches, and the spears. Whichever did this will bear the marks of the struggle."

Japheth retreated down the aisle, his footfalls lost in the noise of the menagerie, his torch's glow shrinking in the darkness.

Noah set his own torch in a sconce outside the pen and stood beside the female. The creature's eyes shifted from her mate to Noah and back again. Noah inspected the female for wounds and the creature let him. He found none, but the damage was done. Without a mate, the griffin was doomed anyway.

The female's wail stopped. Noah watched the animal draw up, stiffen. It snorted. There was a scratching sound beside them. Noah turned. One of the male griffin's back paws raked the wood. His tail rose and slapped the deck. The male tried to lift his head despite the deep wounds in his neck. It lolled to the side, cracked against the deck, then came up again in a lazy semi-circle. Straw stuck to his face. Noah saw there was no blood seeping from the wounds, no sign of a heartbeat in the male, no draw of breath.

The male griffin was both dead and animate.

Beside Noah, the female was stone. Only her dark eyes moved. She followed the odd progress of her companion. The male struggled to get unsteady legs working in concert. The female snorted again, sampling the air.

The male drew upright. His gyrations stopped. He cocked his head to one side. Eyes the color of old milk fixed their lifeless gaze on Noah and the female. His beak parted and he hissed a griffin cry, but strangled, as if bubbling through mud. Around Noah, the menagerie's din dropped to nothing.

The male stepped, lurched, stepped again. He huffed at Noah's scent. Noah caught his breath. Noah willed himself to be invisible. He couldn't fight the male, even in the griffin's wounded state. As a weapon, the torch was more of a threat to the ark than anything else.

The male lunged at Noah, a crooked step. His beak flashed in Noah's vision and Noah thought he saw the face of Death. Then Noah was in the air, knocked aside by the sweep of the female's wing. He fell hard to the deck. He shuffled backwards through straw and filth. It hurt to force breath into his lungs.

The female screamed. Feathered wings sliced the air. She reared back, claws poised. The male lumbered forward, a slow-motion parody of new life. As clumsy as his steps were, his jaws were still swift. He snapped his beak when he lunged, missed when the female side-stepped. She knocked him down and pinned him with a step that shook the deck.

The male flailed against the pressure. His claws made fresh divots in the wood.

Noah expected the female to strike with her beak. The griffin was a beak-hunter by nature. The female defied his wisdom. She rested her weight on the flailing male's back with one foreleg. Her other claw dug into the already-ragged flesh of the male's neck, shredding it. Bones snapped like saplings. The male bucked, bit at the air, tried to roll over, unconcerned he was being mauled.

The female raised her claw a final time and tore through the wet flesh, severing the male's head. It rolled to the side of the aisle. His body fell limp again.

The enclosure was silent as a tomb.

The female retreated a step from the broken body. She looked down at the male's head. Sniffed. Watched. Then she lay beside her mate, stretched her neck, and began to wail again.

Running footfalls drew Noah's gaze from the griffins. He stood and brushed the dirt from his frock. Torchlight swelled as Japheth drew near, followed by Shem and Ham. They studied the grim tableau before them. Japheth stared at the severed head. "Father?"

Noah turned him by the shoulder from the carnage. "Japheth, retrieve two of the axes. The spears may not be enough. Tell the women to stay above this deck. We must inspect every pen and account for every animal, and with great haste."

~o~

The design of the ark worked in their favor. Each deck was self-contained, grouping the animals roughly by size, largest on the lowest deck, smallest on the top. From the wounds Noah saw, whatever felled the griffin was too large to traverse the vertical hatches fore and aft, passages sized for men.

Each deck was designed with concentric ring walkways lined with animal pens and cut-throughs from ring to ring at regular intervals. At the center of each deck was an exercise pen for the beasts.

Because of the size of the deck's residents, the level holding the griffins held only one pen-lined ring requiring search.

The four men inspected the supply storage area to the rear of the deck. The door was sealed, undamaged. Then Noah divided their party into pairs. Noah chose Japheth to remain with him, sending Ham with Shem. Each pair took a spear and an axe.

"Proceed toward the front of the ark," Noah said. "Inspect every pen. Account for every pair of animals. We will meet at the corridor into the exercise pen at mid-ship and share what we discover. From here, there is only one way around, so nothing can get behind us without our notice."

"What if a beast is missing?" There was apprehension in Ham's voice.

"If one is missing, take note of it. If you find one wounded as the male griffin, observe it. If its eyes are white as the griffin's were, and if it is violent, remove its head."

They separated down their respective paths. Noah and Japheth walked in silence. In every pen, the animals were restless. The gorillas cowered by the rear wall. The elephants trumpeted as Noah passed, but Noah didn't know if it was a salute or a warning.

Japheth tugged Noah's sleeve. "There, father." He pointed with the spear at an oily slick on the deck. It was blood, seeping into the aisle from an enclosure ahead.

The basilisks were dead. The two of them lay in confused coils atop each other, their slick scales glistening black and purple in the torchlight. Both of them evidenced deep wounds and excessive bleeding.

Noah was heartsick. The basilisk was fiercely intelligent. Noah knew several of them conversant in his tongue, without the guile or deception of their smaller cousins, the serpents. He'd enjoyed the conversation of the male selected for the voyage, both before the deluge began and after they launched.

"Look at their heads," Noah said.

The skull of each beast had been fractured, opened. The flickering torch cast weird shadows inside the cavities where the creatures' brains should have been. In each were only small crumbles of gray tissue and pools of dark, coagulating blood.

"Do we need to...?" Japheth's voice trailed off, the question completed by holding out the axe.

"It is better to be safe," Noah said.

"Shall I?" Noah saw Japheth wasn't eager for the task.

"They are my responsibility. If I am wrong about our actions, it shall be my error, not yours." He took the axe from his grateful son's hand and stepped around the pools of blood thickening on the deck.

~o~

When they reached the mid-point, Japheth and Ham stood watch on their respective corridors while Noah and Shem investigated the large exercise pen. Shem brought unpleasant news from his side of the vessel. The amphisbaenas, the two-headed serpents, were both dead, their brains consumed. The sun dragons were undead, but had remained confined to their pens. "We destroyed them," Shem said without pride.

"The manticores have also fallen," Noah said, "one undead, one devoured." He swung his torch, eradicating shadows before them. "What kills a creature with three rows of teeth as sharp as blades?"

"Father," Shem said, "something puzzles me. Whatever has done this unspeakable thing selects victims. It could have slower beasts, easier prey. A lion is only a third the predator a manticore is, but the lions are untouched. Why would the monster we seek fight and kill a griffin or a basilisk when it could have an easy time of an elephant or giant sloth?"

Noah's torch hissed, the flame consuming oil. *Because it*

68

is a test, he thought. *God has beset us with deviltry in order to test our wits, our resolve.*

Noah had passed time while building the ark in debate with the basilisk over God's machinations, the coming deluge, and the task of assembling pairs of animals.

"He would not announce the complete test to you," the basilisk argued, coiled around the branches of an olive tree beneath which Noah worked, a canopy of violet scales. "What you think is your trial is but an element of the trial."

Noah sawed in the desert heat. "Building the vessel, collecting the animals, caring for them—I see the elements of the trial very well."

"You overlook something. Something basic."

Noah stopped. He took a drink from the bucket. "Enlighten me."

"Ours is a God of sacrifice. Of offering. He is sacrificing the world entire to renew it. Do you think He will not challenge you to do the same just because you've done what He has asked?"

They debated for some time. Noah was impressed by the basilisk's knowledge and discourse. The creature was more intelligent than some of the men Noah knew.

Noah stopped. The griffin's protective manner. The conversant nature of the basilisk. The cunning of the manticore.

"Their intelligence," he said. "They are all among the highest of the beasts, possessed of mind and reason. It is killing the most intelligent beasts first." He looked at Shem with fresh alarm. "We must get to the unicorns."

~o~

The unicorns were housed near the front of the ark. Noah and his sons continued their separate paths, the count abandoned, their pace doubled.

The unicorns were, in their way, the most advanced of the

69

beasts. Graceful, capable of communication through projected thought, empathic, empowered to charm and heal–theirs was a richness of design. It spoke of the place they held in God's esteem.

Noah was still fifty yards from the pen of the unicorns when an equine shriek filled the air. As Noah and Japheth drew closer, their torches lighted a scene of carnage.

Both the male and female unicorn were stained ocher, blood matted in their fine coats, crusted to their horns. The sounds they made were not the melodic neighs familiar to Noah. These were touched with madness. Both animals displayed the same milky white eyes as the male griffin.

The shriek in the darkness was not from either of the unicorns, but the female pegasus. She was under siege by the female unicorn at the mouth of the pegasus pen. The unicorn feinted with her horn and snapped her jaws, trying to pierce the pegasus's breast. Already wounded, the pegasus struggled with wing and hooves to hold off her undead opponent.

Behind them in the pen, the male pegasus lay motionless on the deck. Noah watched the male unicorn leverage his horn against the fallen beast's skull. It tore away the flesh. It cracked and pierced the skull. A wedge of bone clattered off the rear wall of the pen. The male unicorn lowered his maw and began to feast on brain matter.

The fight of the females spilled into the aisle, almost trampling Shem and Ham. Seeing the men, the pegasus fought with renewed vigor against the reanimate unicorn, her wings battering the sides of the creature's head.

"Quickly," Noah said, and directed Shem towards the pen. Shem and Ham maneuvered inside. Caught up in his feeding, the male unicorn gave them little notice. Ham drove his spear into the unicorn's throat, trying to topple him off his feet.

The male snarled, long and low. He pulled his bloody mouth from the skull. Shem slammed the blunt edge of the axe into the side of the unicorn's head. Then he turned his wrists and brought the blade down on the unicorn's neck. The creature's flesh split to the bone. Shem finished him with a second swing.

If the female unicorn noticed the decapitation of her mate, she never turned from her assault on the remaining pegasus. The tip of her horn tore a hole in the left wing of the great horse. The pegasus stumbled and fell. The unicorn clopped forward, lips skinned off her teeth. Noah drove his spear into the right foreleg of the unicorn, breeching the joint. The bronze tip snapped bone and cartilage with a crackle. The unicorn pulled up lame. She turned her lifeless eyes on Noah. Blood ran in dark rivulets from the base of the horn down the beast's face. Noah could feel the unicorn's mind in his, distorting his thoughts, trying to

adriftforeverstormneverending
plant images, instill doubt
forsakenforgottensacrificed
with her mind. Noah shivered. He saw the bodies of his sons, the women, himself, bones wrapped in their garments, prone on the deck of the ark as it listed on the endless rolling sea. He could feel the emptiness, the absence of God, abandoned by the Creator to the storm of His making.

Noah felt a weight of despair. His arm went slack. The spear dropped from his hand.

The unicorn stepped towards Noah and lowered her chin, angling her horn at Noah's head.

A flash of metal glittered in the torchlight. There was a wet thud and the unicorn screamed. The beast's head drooped at an unnatural angle. The sight of the axe wound cleaved in the beast's neck shook Noah from his stupor. He watched Japheth bring the axe down a second time. The unicorn's scream stopped as her head fell to the deck. The again-dead body collapsed beside it. The axe slipped from Japheth's hands and clattered on the wood. He dropped to his knees in the straw and began to weep.

The female pegasus tried to rise and failed. She collapsed and rolled onto her side. One wing twitched, useless. Her breathing was labored, thick.

Noah retrieved his spear. He stroked the suffering beast's nose. The pegasus calmed. Noah drove a merciful spear through the animal's heart. He retrieved the axe from beside Japheth and wiped the blade clean before severing the magnificent, unfortunate creature's head.

~o~

It was a dark dawn, the rain harder than the day before.

Noah and his sons inspected each animal on the deck. As they worked, Shem told his father, "The female unicorn was wounded before she came aboard, a bite on her side. She was the only female to be found. I believed it would heal. If I had known–"

"You cannot blame yourself," Noah said. He hoped whatever wounded the unicorn was already dead by God's design.

Alone in the exercise pen, when the inspection was complete, Noah beseeched God for a reason why *these* creatures were taken. He lamented his failure to protect the beasts lost, asked God to tell him what to do, prayed the animals might be returned whole, so Noah might better prove his stewardship.

The only answer was the creak of the deck and the murmur of the remaining animals.

Noah's sons waited by the unicorn pen for Noah to return. When he did, his face was grim, eyes fixed in both determination and grief. "We cannot leave the flesh to rot."

Japheth looked from his brothers to Noah. "Father, we should also make an offering."

Noah felt a flash of anger. "And what species would you have me condemn? They are paired male and female to repopulate–"

Noah stopped, overtaken by grim clarity.

~o~

The saws and axes saw much use. The doors of the now-empty pens were cut away and taken to the top deck of the ship. In the rain, Japheth fashioned an altar from them.

Noah widened the hatchways between decks. The largest creatures had entered through doors in the hull that now held back the sea. The size limitation of the hatches kept the unicorns contained, but also worked against easy removal of the dead beasts.

Ham and Shem performed in silence the grisly duty of sawing and chopping, reducing creatures of marvel and wonder to chunks of flesh and bone. They took care to protect themselves from the blood of the animals. The remains were piled into baskets and hauled, deck by deck, to the top level of the vessel.

When the dead beasts were removed, Noah walked alone to the griffin's pen. There was no struggle when Noah slipped the rope around her neck and led her to the ladder to the deck above. He'd prepared rope and pulley, but there was no need. The griffin climbed on her own.

Outside the family's enclosure, pelted by the storm, Noah prayed, the tears in his eyes indiscernible from the driving rain. The griffin lay upon the altar. Her mane and feathered wings were slick, wet. She kept her eyes closed.

Noah tried to ignore the beast had saved his life. The words of the basilisk echoed in his mind. *Sacrifice.* Did sacrifice have to feel like betrayal?

He prayed aloud to God, equal measures of atonement for his failure and thanks they were not all consumed by the evil placed among them. He unsheathed his knife. He slit the griffin's throat and made of the beast a sacrifice. Blood flowed to the deck and became one with the rain.

One after another, the grisly parts of the fallen species were cast over the rail by Noah's sons. The griffin was last. It took all four men to consign the beautiful corpse to the rolling floodwaters. Noah stood at the rail when they were done, staring at the sea.

From beneath the eaves of the enclosure, the cries of the seagulls mingled with his sobs.

–o–

FEAR #7

FEAR #7 HAS OCCURRED to me, and it is unspeakable.

It slipped in through an unguarded moment, vinegar and bloody-iron across the tongue. Even though I know it's not real, like the six manifestations before it, I can't stop myself from responding as if it is.

Spiro Durante is the source. Garner & Fitch bought his building, a century-old, ten-story slide zone. It's the last piece of a redevelopment puzzle that's cost me nights, weekends, my kid's attention, my wife's affections. Sleeping alone on the sofa with the wool cushions was going to be worth it. They'd make me a partner. I'd swim in coins like Scrooge McDuck. Enough money to soothe the kid's bent soul, to mend marital fences—or survive tearing them out.

Except for Durante in the penthouse, not one tenant pushed back. They took buyouts like they came with free groceries. I didn't gather until later: they didn't so much want out of their homes as they wanted away from him.

Fitch sent me in when the third offer letter 'refused by

addressee' returned in the mailbag. "Scrape him off like a tick," Fitch said. I'd done it before. Holdouts in the Greenscape corridor, pension widows rooted in crumbling rooms. So I went.

Durante met me at his door before I could ring, like he knew. Things from four corners of seven continents were crammed into the penthouse. It could have been the world's attic. Sunlight through grimy windows laid a sepia patina over everything. He'd been the tenant as far back as we could find records, but didn't look a day over forty, except for his eyes. Green, the color of a swamp swallowing logs. Something ancient crouched behind them. It had cut the straight-razor smile in his face. I could smell it, poison in a flesh suit. Waiting. Wanting.

I understood the eagerness of the other tenants. I refused coffee or tea. I wanted to present the offer and get out. Came on strong. Told him we'd have the cops drag him out, demo the place with all his knick-knacks inside. Intimidation. Menace. He was a pothole that needed paving.

He pushed the deal back, unread. "I will decide when I move on."

"We don't have to offer you anything. Your lease was severed with the sale. This is generosity for your inconvenience."

"Let me explain generosity." He motioned with his left hand, a slow sign language. The garnet ring on his finger seemed to flicker. "Seven fears will occur to you and your masters. New fears. Things you've never before given a second thought. Things that will consume you from within. And *then* I will move on."

"You're poorly positioned for threats."

His laughter rumbled from an ancient grave. "You mistake a guarantee."

I called the office on my way out, set eviction wheels in motion.

That night was the spider. I've never been afraid of them. One as big as my torso slid from under the couch, mossy green lines on its slick, black body. Tree-limb legs. In the shadows, heart pounding, I beat it down with a chair. It died screeching. But when I turned on the lights, it was a quarter-sized spot mangled under a broken chair. The wife thought I'd snapped. But the kid saw, mentioned the weird green lines on its tiny, broken body. On some level, I knew it had happened.

Fears blossomed one after another over the next four days. Fear of falling, my office floor collapsed into a chasm, ring of green fire at the bottom. I screamed and clutched the desk until Maggie came in to check on me, crossed the same floor the office always had. Fear of darkness, seeping into the subway car from the tunnel. Monstrosities within writhed and snapped at me before the train returned to the surface, other riders recoiling from what they believed a fit. Fear of strangers, in the form of a scrawny homeless who rattled and grew into a muscled hulk with a club when I refused him change. Fear of dogs, a pack with green eyes and rotten meat on their breath that cornered me in the park. Except they were three leashed terriers, their confused owner trying to understand my shouts.

I fared better than Garner. Three days after Durante's glamour, the old man screamed "I'm sorry!" at no one and threw himself twenty stories to the sidewalk. Fritch was babbling about nuclear war when they buckled him in a wrap-around jacket and called Bellevue.

In their absence, I got the damned job done. Cops followed me to Durante's door, court order in hand. The penthouse was empty save for an index card tacked to the fireplace mantle. Block letters. OUR REVELS ARE ENDED. Then the police discussed whether to shoot me and leave me for the rats, or to devour me themselves. I ran. They called after me, confused.

When I got home, the wife was at her book club. I popped a beer and tussled the kid's hair. He set out with his friend Donnie to the market Donnie's father ran a few blocks away.

Choice cuts, cured meats. I wondered what the kid got out of the place. That's when fear #7 occurred.

It's coming up the elevator soon. Dull cleaver, rusted bone saw, crooked steel pins, other bits. My son. But it won't be my son. It isn't eleven, doesn't want me to work less or go to little league games. It will wear my boy's body, a hint of Spiro Durante green in its eyes. When it arrives, it will gnash and snarl, chop and slice. It will only be my son again when it's dead.

But I'm not afraid of him. I'm afraid of myself.

Fear #7 is what I will do to my son to survive.

And it is unspeakable.

—o—

Every Hero An Hombre, Every Wolf A Clown

HECTOR TOASTED WITH *ARROQUENO* mezcal brought in from Oaxaca by the bar's owner. "To the new heavyweight champion of Luchadores Club!"

"This week, anyway!" Alex added.

Ramon grinned. The gold-buckled belt hung over the back of his bar stool, trophy of Ojos Rojos' victory over El Ruiseñor an hour before. "Gracias, amigos. Salute!"

They clinked glasses, sipped liquid fire. Only gringo frat boys shot mezcal.

Luchadores Club met in a Quonset hut beside Marco's Bar on Jerry Street. Unless rust over the door counted, the building had no sign. It didn't need one. Neighbors for blocks around packed the place twice a week to watch *lucha libre* wrestlers grapple and drop-kick for a cut of the gate. It was half the price of a movie, twice as much fun. If the city cared, concern ended at insurance requirements and the occasional parking ticket.

Hector was El Lobo Gran Malo–The Big Bad Wolf. Dark gray and black trunks, matching Chuck Taylor sneakers with extra-high tops that reached mid-calf, a gray mask with yellow trim around the eyes, and jagged white trim–teeth, if you please–around the mouth. He used three signature moves: Huff, Puff, and Blow. He loved hearing the crowd chant *"Soplas la casa abajo!"*–Blow the house down!–when he laid the third move on his opponents.

Ramon set his glass, asked Hector, "Has Emilio decided what he wants for his party yet?"

"No." Emilio was Hector's son, on the cusp of turning nine. "He's gone through twenty ideas. Batman. Star Wars. Iron Man. Something called Minecraft. He's come up with stuff I didn't even know was stuff."

"Kids love the luchadores," Alex hinted. Alex wrestled as El Loco Hombre Azul–the Crazy Blue Man. Crazy about being a luchador, Hector figured. It was Alex's answer for everything. Flat tire? Call a luchador. Termite problem? Call a luchador.

"It's Emilio's choice. He's never expressed interest in a party with friends before, so he's getting whatever he wants."

"What's wrong with luchadores?" Like Alex had been passed over for a promotion. Labor dispute? Call a luchador.

"Nothing. He's a kid. Kids have lots of choices. But he needs to decide soon. Three weeks isn't much time to set something up."

Alex snorted. "Three *hours*, you could have a half-dozen wrestlers."

~o~

It was after dark when Hector pulled into his driveway. From the porch, Lydia fixed him with a glance learned from her *abuela*. She swore it wasn't the evil eye. It looked evil enough.

"You have a problem," she said as he reached the steps.

"It was just a couple mezcals with the guys."

"Not booze. The boy. He's chosen his party entertainment. Came out of his room, said, 'Mama, I've made my decision,' and gave me this." She handed Hector a folded sheet of paper.

"That's not a problem. It's an answered prayer."

"Maybe if mass was held at the Improv."

Hector unfolded it. Black letters in a sea of white bond declared:

XYLO THE CLOWN

Hector studied his wife. "You're messing with me."

"No."

"C'mon. This isn't funny."

"Billy Miller told Emilio about the clown at his party. Balloon animals. Magic tricks. The folding xylophone."

"The confetti cannon?"

"On and on about the confetti cannon."

Hector rubbed the back of his neck. "Do you think Emilio knows?"

"No. I think you're a victim of your own showmanship." Lydia opened the door. Her voice dropped. "And that big lie you live."

"'Lie' is such an ugly word."

Hector followed her. Inside, his daughters Katie and Elizabeth python-hugged his legs.

~o~

In Peninsula, Texas–incorporated 1872 along the Guadalupe River, population 254,000–luchadores and clowns did not mix.

Peninsula birthed one of the first rodeo clown schools in Texas, circa 1903. Before long, the program expanded to include circus and independent performers. Their clowns could be found everywhere. Two of Barnum and Bailey's boss clowns passed through Peninsula zip codes.

By contrast, the city didn't meet *lucha libre* until after World War Two, when Salvador Lutteroth's traveling exhibition from Mexico City passed through on its way to Houston. The acrobatics, the pageantry, the unashamed fun–the descendants of Mexico cleaved to it. Two recreational leagues popped up in the months following Lutteroth's visit.

A few still recalled the League Night Fracas of 1961 at the AMF lanes on Brazos Street, but the original sleight was lost to history. Whether clowns believed their livelihood impinged upon or luchadores felt marginalized, the blood between them ran black. They entertained in their own neighborhoods and kept to their own sides of the street. No one was bold enough–or stupid enough–to mingle squirting daisies and flying tackles.

Except for Xylo the Clown. El Lobo Gran Malo. Hector Ramirez, plumber.

~o~

Lost in the shuffle of six children, Hector became class cut-up for attention. Acting up shortened to acting, begat drama club, talent shows, roles in local theater productions. He attended LSU, eyes on a dramatic arts degree. When told, his father shook his head and wished Hector luck. "Just never let me see you in tights."

Xylo, outfitted in a lime green jacket and ruffled shirt, baggy pants and oversized shoes, was born at LSU. Tuition, fees, textbooks, meals–those demanded every piece of change. One professor suggested greasepaint as a sidelight. "You can read a room. You're a natural entertainer."

With five siblings, Hector knew his way around a birthday party. Working them as an entertainer felt natural. Laughter

82

and applause were lagniappe. It beat scrubbing dishes in the dining hall. Dirty cookware didn't applaud.

Xylo went into a box when Hector met Lydia, was a wistful memory by the time they settled in Peninsula with two kids. He met Ramon on the job with Palmer Plumbing. Ramon introduced him to *lucha libre*. Hector was a cruiserweight, took to the acrobatics with gusto. It was a year before he even heard about issues with clowns.

Then the economy tanked, killed by the announcement that Lydia was pregnant again. Hector scoured classified ads, seeking another job for months before stumbling across Xylo's box while cleaning the garage.

Parties paid well. Weekends were typically free. Both wrestling and clowning covered his face. Hector mapped where it was safe to perform as Xylo when not appearing as the Wolf. His double life worked without a hitch for three years until Billy Miller, third grade braggart, soured the deal.

~o~

Hector knocked outside Emilio's open door. The boy glanced from a web page about the Aztecs, smart brown eyes reading Hector from behind gold-rimmed glasses. He frowned. "Mama told you."

"Yeah."

"You mad?"

Hector sat on the bed. Old springs squeaked. "No. Why would I be?"

"Because I want a clown for my party, not a luchador."

"I'm not mad. Surprised, maybe. You really like wrestling."

"Yeah. But the guys know all the wrestlers, like how you're Big Bad Wolf, and King Bee is Cousin Juan. It's not as much fun. I want something... different."

"Different isn't always better."

"How come 'different' is always better when Mama cooks something weird?"

"Because she's Mama."

"Anyway, Billy Miller knows cool clowns. He goes to the circus every summer. And a clown at a luchador's house? The guys will talk about it for weeks!"

And there it was. When you're nine, you want to impress the guys. Too soon, Hector thought, it would be about impressing girls instead. His left eye twitched at the notion. "It's your birthday. You want a clown? You get a clown."

"Thanks."

"You sure you want this Xylo? He sounds kinda goofy."

Emilio turned back to his computer. "They all would to you. You're not allowed to like clowns. It might be a law."

~o~

"Did Juan bang your head into a turnbuckle again?" Lydia snapped off the lamp and snuggled against her husband.

"No, really. I know how I can perform at the party."

"In two hours, you've got a plan?"

"A bulletproof plan."

"Wow. Luchador, clown, criminal mastermind. My mother was wrong. I *did* hit the jackpot."

"The week of the party, when I'm around Emilio, I'll mention it's my on-call weekend."

"It's not."

"He won't know that. The day of the party, an hour before, I'll get called in. I'll have my props in the van. I'll drive around the block, suit up, and come back on foot as Xylo. I'll do the gig, leave, clean up, come back, and no one's the wiser."

Despite the dark, he could feel Lydia staring at him again. It was a strange sensation. Prickly. "Suppose the other luchadores show up to play 'Suplex the Clown'?"

84

"I'm going to encourage them to come. They're my brothers. They'll posture, but none of them will come intending to start a ruckus. They'll let the clown take the first swing, which he'll never do."

"Won't they figure out you're not on-call and not at the party? Doesn't some little thing always reveal a secret identity?"

"They'll be too busy fretting about a clown."

Lydia was quiet for a time. "Emilio will be upset if you're not there."

"He's nine. He's elastic."

"And you don't think he'll recognize you?"

"Kids fall for this all the time. Look at Clark Kent and Superman."

Lydia kissed his neck, under the ear. "Except Superman *is* bulletproof."

~o~

Commotion ensued at practice the next night, word spreading about Emilio's clown. Hector was the Lawrence Olivier of Jerry Street: exasperated luchador and long-suffering father, trying to make his child happy. He played on their sympathies, begged their indulgence. "Don't let Emilio's party go bust. Let your kids come. If you're really concerned, hang around to see the show."

Everyone manned-up in Hector's time of need. Even Alex, who had no children. "I just want to see this joker up close."

~o~

Emilio's frown was the Grand Canyon the day of the party, when Hector grabbed his tool belt from the peg beside the door. "But I wanted you to see him."

"Mama will shoot video. If I'm late, we'll watch it

together tonight." He tussled Emilio's hair. It brought the boy no solace. "I'll try to be quick, but it sounds like a pretty bad leak."

Emilio half-smiled. "Will you come in your mask?"

"Sure. Then you can have a luchador *and* a clown."

Having both proved a non-issue. When Xylo the Clown entered the yard through the side gate an hour later, eleven masked faces greeted him with grim silence. The luchadores formed a row before the tall wooden fence, arms crossed, jaws firm. They returned neither Xylo's smile nor wave. They might have been wrestling-themed lawn ornaments.

Xylo was setting up on the deck when Lydia motioned him to the side yard. Xylo shuffled down the steps and across the yard, rocking side to side.

"Did you call the cavalry?" Lydia pointed up the street.

A dozen clowns ambled single-file down the sidewalk, a rainbow waiting to be curved across the sky. Hector recognized several of them: Sprinkles, Polka Dot, Clapper. The others were strangers, but the show of solidarity was unmistakable.

Led by Sprinkles, they marched up the driveway to the side gate. Sprinkles tipped his neon blue bowler hat to Lydia, gloomy. "Good day, ma'am. We understand one of our brethren is performing here."

Xylo waved. Sprinkles grinned and waved back, then grew dour again. "We also understand there are luchadores present."

"Yes. Friends of my husband."

"We're here to ensure there are no unfortunate incidents."

"Oh, everyone's on best behavior."

"With your permission, we'd like to tarry in your driveway until Xylo's done, and afford him safe passage home."

Lydia bit her lip to tame her smile. "It's your show, Xylo."

Xylo gave Sprinkles a thumbs-up. "See you soon!" he squeaked, a cartoon. He could feel an unfunny sweat on his brow.

~o~

Maybe it was the pressure, but Hector gave the best performance of Xylo the Clown's life. The children clapped, stomped their feet, whistled in all the right places. Lydia and the other mothers shouted encouragement while tending the party.

The luchadores were non-committal, eyes like hawks in the holes of their masks. Only Alex tried to stir the pot, when Xylo unfolded his namesake instrument. Xylo cupped his hand to his ear, asked the kids for requests. They shouted classics: "Old MacDonald," "This Old Man," "Pop Goes the Weasel."

From the back, Alex called, "'El Carretero'." The luchadores chuckled.

Xylo pointed at Alex and nodded, excited. He licked a gloved fingertip, tested the breeze. He gripped the two mallets, raised them, and banged out a simple version of the Mexican folk song with which Alex had tried to stump him.

The kids cheered. Cowed, Alex leaned against the fence. Hector caught Ramon smiling.

Xylo fired the confetti cannon to a hearty ovation. He led a chorus of "Happy Birthday" for Emilio. Mothers dished ice cream and cake. The kids ate around a long table set up under a tent, and Xylo packed, the show complete.

He'd secured the cannon when Lydia stopped beside him. "Emilio's miserable."

Xylo squeaked, "Didn't he enjoy the show?"

Words worse than any body slam. "Yes. But he thinks his father skipped the party because of the clown."

"Where is he?"

Lydia tipped her head towards Emilio, sitting alone, sullen, poking cake with a plastic fork.

Xylo sashayed across the yard and sat beside the boy.

"What's wrong, Emilio?"

"My dad missed the party."

"I'm sure he'll be here soon."

The boy shook his head, fine strands of hair waving at the sun. "I think he's mad at me because I wanted you at my party. He said it was okay, but then he said he had to work. He's not even on-call. I checked his calendar."

In Hector's head, Lydia mouthed the word "bulletproof".

"Your act was great," Emilio continued, "but I guess I wanted my dad here more."

The sadness in his son's voice was a nail through Hector's heart. No ruse was worth it.

"Emilio, can you keep a secret?"

Emilio glanced, curious. Xylo unzipped the fanny pack slung around his waist. He withdrew the luchador mask, the face of El Lobo Gran Malo, and handed it to the boy.

Emilio turned it in his hands, studied it. Glanced at Xylo, then the mask again. Hector waited for the boy to connect the dots. Then Emilio shouted, loud enough to be heard on the other side of the neighbor's house, "What did you do to my dad!?!"

~o~

One seldom witnesses the instant all Hell breaks loose. Recording a tender father/son moment, Lydia caught one on video.

Emilio bolts from the chair. Runs to the luchadores, screaming, waving El Lobo's face like a battle flag.

The luchadores see the mask in Emilio's hand. A luchador's mask is his identity. They know El Lobo would never willingly surrender it, especially to a clown.

"What did you do, you *payaso bastardo*?" Alex shouts. The luchadores advance.

Hearing the budding commotion, the clowns in the

driveway become a Technicolor wave into the yard.

Children scatter, mobile air-raid sirens.

Pockets of chaos bloom like flowers. Luchadores launch themselves. Wigs fly. Clowns leap on wrestler backs, steer them by the eye-holes in masks. Ramon headlocks Sprinkles, crushes his bowler. Polka Dot levels Alex with the meanest left hook ever thrown by a lady clown.

Xylo stands on a chair and shouts, squeaky lilt replaced by Hector's voice. Commanding. Resonant. Terrified. "Knock it off! Stop! All of you!" The chaos abates, but doesn't end until he adds, "Do you want the neighbors to call the cops?"

When he has their attention, Xylo rips the lime green wig from his head, pulls the matching bulb from his nose, and drops them on the ground. "It's me! Hector! I'm fine! *I'm* Xylo the Clown! Everyone relax!"

For a moment, everything stops. Hector starts to explain when Alex cries, "I won't let them convert you!" He knocks Hector from the chair with a flying tackle.

That's when Lydia stops recording.

~o~

"I can't believe you missed my speech."

"It's been four days," Lydia said. "Let it go."

"Maybe after you travel back in time and record it."

"The exciting part was over."

Hector sipped his beer with braced wrist. "At least all the injuries were minor. No one got arrested. We probably won't get sued. And some good came out of it."

"Good?" Lydia toweled a plate dry. "Suspended by the Brotherhood of Clowns *and* Luchadores Club. None of them are even speaking to you."

"See? I untied them against a common foe." He took another sip. "The Brotherhood won't pass me gigs, but they can't stop me from performing. It's not a union. The guys will come around. Ramon's more hurt by me keeping a secret than anything."

"No, but Marco can keep you out of the ring."

"Marco's a businessman. He'll make me a villain for a while. *El Payaso Lobo*. The Clown Wolf. It's like being in a sideshow."

"Understatement of the year." Lydia stacked plates in the cupboard, hung the damp dishtowel on a hook, and hugged Hector around the shoulders. "You're a good man, Hector. But that was a lot of hassle for a birthday party. Was it really worth it?"

Emilio popped into the doorway, grin and waving hands, Kermit the Frog with a bowl haircut. "The Luchadores vs Clowns video just reached 500,000 hits on YouTube! I think it got linked by Boing-Boing. It even has a comment from some guy in the Maldives. I don't even know where that is!" Then he was gone again, down the hall with a whoop, his sisters joining him in the joyful chorus that filled the house end-to-end.

Hector glanced at Lydia, lips curled in a smile. "I'm sorry. What was your question?"

–o–

TO THE DEVIL, A GOAT

Gordie sighed and shifted his position, crunching leaves under his feet, and glared at Bobby. "This is the dumbest thing you've ever talked me into."

As if in agreement with Gordie, the goat they'd staked beside the tree bleated.

"My grandpa never lied," Bobby said. He cast a glance to the west. The lowest arc of the sun, muzzy from the veil of clouds, had touched the horizon. "As soon as the sun sets, he'll come out of that hole."

They'd cleared the kaleidoscope of fallen leaves to expose the hollow. It dipped deep under the old maple tree. Both tree and hole had been there as long as anyone could recall, south of town, where the roads to the four compass points crossed. It was narrow, just wide enough to accommodate a grown man if he wriggled. But even with a spider web of roots to climb down, no one explored it, not even in the summers when the pond went dry from the heat and the kids crazy from boredom.

The maple was left alone. Old timers told stories.

Billy's grandpa was an old timer.

"Balls he will," Gordie said. He spat onto the dusty ground. "The devil don't live under that tree."

"No, he don't," Billy agreed. "He lives in Hell. But once a year, he comes to earth, at the moment the sun sets on the equinox, when scales tip in favor of night. He takes a sacrifice. Then he roams through the night."

"Everyone knows his night is Halloween."

Billy looked Gordie straight in the eyes, his gaze cool. "Everyone don't know anything."

The sun was halfway past the horizon. Its light washed everything pink. "What about up at the north pole, where the night goes for six months?" Gordie asked.

"No holes in the tundra." Billy coiled a second length of chain around his arm. It was silver, the same as the chain that tethered the goat. The goat bleated again as if to offer advice on Billy's technique. "You can go if you're scared."

Gordie snorted and held his ground. He was the biggest of the sophomore kids, and already played left tackle for the varsity football team. "And miss my chance to laugh at you?"

"You won't be laughing when we catch him," Billy said, and widened the choke chain at the end of his coil. "He's got powers. There's lots a guy can do with that."

Getting the goat had been easy enough. Old Man Hansen's stock was always wandering out of his barns. No one would miss it. It was only going to wind up slaughtered anyway. The chains had been dunked in holy water, an abuse of altar boy Billy's access to the church that he felt was justified. You couldn't catch the devil without something blessed.

Billy stood like a cowboy, feet apart, coil of chain ready. "When he goes for the goat, I'll get the loop over his head. Then you have to help me tie him good."

"Uh huh. Soon as you lasso him."

Billy looked over his shoulder, watched the last sliver of

sun as it vanished below the horizon. "Get ready!" He glanced at Gordie, but Gordie was already staring at the hole, his eyes crinkled in a squint. Billy turned.

A girl was climbing from the darkness. Billy guessed she was no older than nine or ten. There was dirt smudged on her cheeks and around her dark eyes. Her hair was matted, unwashed. Billy saw her checkered dress was tattered along the hem, snagged and torn. She was sobbing as she crawled onto the dirt and leaves from within the hollow. She looked from Gordie to Billy.

"Help me," she said. "I fell in there."

Billy set the chain aside and walked to the girl. He helped her up. She tried to straighten her soiled dress, sniffling.

"I was walking," she said, dazed, "and fell right through the leaves. I don't know when." She coughed and dirt crumbled from her hair. "I'm Lucy."

"I'm Billy. This is Gordie." Billy studied the girl. Grime was packed under her fingernails. Her hands were raw from climbing the roots out of the hole. His task forgotten, he offered the girl a smile. "It'll be okay."

"Will you walk me home?" she asked, and both boys nodded. It was the right thing to do, Billy thought. The girl was trembling in the twilight. She seemed to be in shock.

"Sure. Where do you live?"

"This way," Lucy said, and offered her hands. Billy took one in his, and Gordie took the other.

As she led them towards the hollow, Billy was forgetting something, but he couldn't recall what, even as the vise-like grip on his hand pulled him into darkness, even as his bones snapped and the mingled smells of offal and sulfur filled his nostrils. *Something*, he thought. *Something about a lasso.*

The old tree shook. Branches groaned and fell silent.

Alone, the goat bleated in the gathering dusk.

—o—

One Man's Famine

HE WAITED AS HE had each day for the two weeks preceding, the intermittent growl in his stomach growing more regular. He cupped his eyes and peered through the plate glass, shielding out the reflection of the city, the irrelevant city, now as vacant as a church on Thursday–the silent edifices, the meaningless facades of banks and offices, the glassy eyes of empty windows. He shut it all out in favor of the quiet comfort of the darkened interior of Hap's.

Red counter tops, still glistening from their last good scrubbing; swivel stools with the padded seats that hissed when you sat on them; stainless steel contraptions for toasting, mixing, refrigeration; anything you could want from a kitchen, it all waited beyond the glass.

What Mitch wanted was a burger–a greasy, juicy, inch-and-a-half thick patty, ground chuck mixed with some of the little onion bits Hap liked to toss in, topped off with a slab of Wisconsin cheddar that melted until it blended with the juices of the burger and ran onto the potato roll on which it was served. No regular bun for a Hap's burger, no sir. It was a '62 Caddy convertible with leather seats, a prom queen that put out, a Vegas-sized jackpot from an absurdly large slot machine. It was all Mitch wanted.

At the notion of that burger, his stomach growled again, audible in the stillness. He couldn't see the grill, no matter which window he chose. It was in back, hidden away from the prying eyes of customers, critics, and health inspectors alike. Mitch believed that was part of the magic of Hap's burger: you never got to see the trick of how he flavored it. He might dust it with paprika or French onion soup mix. He might fry it in the fat of a freshly killed lamb. For all Mitch knew, the old man mopped his brow twice with the patty before dropping it onto the sizzling grill and setting a weight on it. Mitch didn't care. The flavor, the aroma, the mere fact of Hap's burger was the compelling end, and the means mattered not.

He'd considered smashing the window, going inside, helping himself. Lord knew it wouldn't be the first time this week Mitch had forced a door for a meal. If Hap was still around, that would get the man's ass down here. But the thought Hap would get mad and elect to not serve him raised a shudder in Mitch. He couldn't live without that burger. *Couldn't.*

As Mitch weighed shattering glass versus being thrown from Hap's version of Eden, he felt a tap on his shoulder. "Mitch, man. You're persistent, I'll give you that."

Mitch turned to face Henry. That was all Mitch knew: Henry. He was a tall man, but not to the point of intimidation. A spark of wily intelligence flickered in his eyes. His dark hair was shocked with gray at one temple. They'd run into each other every day this week in front of Hap's, the only evidence of life left around 72nd Street. Henry stayed uptown with three or four other people he'd met since the city went empty. He'd been after Mitch to come with him and join them at the hotel they'd commandeered, offered him safety in numbers. Henry dressed like he was on his way to visit his broker. It made Mitch pull self-consciously at the ratty jeans that were now a size too big.

"He'll be here," Mitch said. "Hap, he's dependable. He had the flu something terrible a few years ago. Laid him up at Mercy Hospital for two weeks. Rents being what they are, Hap being the only cook, losing money every day he was laid up, people thought the place would have to close. No way to make money and pay bills when you're in a bad way. No more Hap's burger! But Hap came back. It's what he does. He's a survivor. A man of the people."

"The people? If there are a dozen left in this whole city, I'd be surprised, and I know half of them," Henry said. "Whatever happened, we're it. We're on our own. Hap isn't coming. Nobody is."

Mitch cupped his eyes and peered inside again. Polished chrome and squared-off stainless steel napkin dispensers beckoned. "Yes he will," he said, defiance in his tone. "You wait. Hap will come. He'll be back making burgers again. Soon, too. And burgers for the faithful first. You'll have to stand in line."

"The power has been off. The meat's all bad, even if Hap was still here, which he isn't."

"You're wrong!" Mitch said, punctuated by his stomach's fresh snarl.

Henry stared at him. "When was the last time you ate?"

Mitch pondered. It was within the last few days, something out of a can he found in the cupboard of a place he broke into in his building. He'd run out of food. He didn't keep much on hand on a normal day. Mrs. Tompkins had vanished with the rest of his neighbors. Mitch considered it less of a sin and more of a necessary blemish, kicking her door in and raiding her cabinets. Whatever it was he'd eaten, it had been insubstantial. He wasn't even sure he'd kept it down. "Don't

97

know. Doesn't matter. I'll be right as rain after that burger."

Henry shook his head. "Look, Mitch. I hardly know you, but there's nothing here for you anymore. You're wasting away. And for what? Some old, pudgy fry cook who disappeared with the rest of the population? Come with me. We'll fix you right up."

Mitch hitched his jeans up again, ran his hand across his flattening stomach, a vacant gesture. "I have to wait for him. I can't miss him. If no one's here, he might not come back again." He stared at the empty stools, sought solace in the way the light reflected off their frames. His voice took on the weight of a cloud. "This is all I got to do on earth, Henry."

Behind him, Henry sighed.

The steel socket wrench caught the sunlight on the downward swing and landed at the base of Mitch's skull with a crack. The force of the blow bounced Mitch off the glass, which rang from the impact. His body crumpled to the ground, spasming on the sidewalk. Henry finished him with two more quick blows.

He stood over the body, studying it. It was a shame how lean Mitch had become this last week, but he'd still go far enough uptown. They'd learned how to stretch a meal.

—o—

THE SHAMAN IN RELIEF

DUST FLEW AND LOOSE stone crunched under the tires as Mathis pulled into the lot in front of the Route 62 Funplex.

He parked beside a silver BMW convertible that seemed to glow in the sunshine. He killed the engine and pulled up the league website on his phone. Twelve days into May and the Cherokees were in the process of dropping their seventh in a row, digging a trench at the bottom of the NL Central. A triple play by the Mets had killed a fourth-inning, bases-loaded, nobody-out rally. Mathis expected Paulson was climbing the walls of the owner's suite.

Mathis pocketed the phone as he entered the Funplex. The teenage girl at the ticket booth glanced over the top of a dog-eared copy of Us Weekly, sized him up with bored brown eyes, and pointed in the direction of the miniature golf course. "Eleventh hole," she said.

"Excuse me?"

She sighed. "You're the baseball man, right?"

Mathis nodded.

"Mister Raines's office is next to the eleventh hole. The one with the Alamo."

~o~

"Baseball Man!" Raines called as if they were old friends. He stood behind his desk and offered his hand. The man was tall and lean, his tan deep. He looked like a vacationing executive: pink Abercrombie & Fitch polo, gray khaki shorts and flip-flops. "Roger Raines."

"Earl Mathis."

"Made it okay, huh? Good."

"This is an interesting set-up," Mathis said. "I was expecting an office building." Mathis had done his homework. Raines made a respectable living in amusements. He owned three locations on the reservation, plus a couple off: go carts, mini golf, batting cages, arcades.

"I like the sound of the kids having fun in the fresh air. Sometimes they shank one off the wall. It reminds me how I got where I am."

"I suppose that's better than a go-cart crashing through the door."

"You don't know how right you are." Raines studied him. Mathis tried to be inscrutable. "My grandfather said I could bring you over when you arrived."

"Do you think he'll accept our offer?"

Raines laughed. "I've stopped trying to figure out what he'll do next." He grabbed his keys from the desk. "But if he doesn't put the whammy on you, you're welcome to come back and play eighteen holes on me."

"You really think he'd curse me?"

"Nah," Raines said. "He's only done it the one time."

100

~o~

Mathis rode in silence in Raines's BMW. The wind was loud with the top down. Raines insisted on going convertible. "There are too few decent days to not do it." The ride was so smooth, Mathis started to nod off. He'd driven a compact all the way from Louisville, ten hours on a budget-grade suspension. Raines's car made even rough two-lane blacktop feel like glass.

"To be honest," Raines said after a while, "I think my grandfather's wasting your time. He takes great pride in what he did. Every year, he throws a party when the Cherokees are statistically eliminated. The man makes a terrific pot of chili."

"Has he ever told you why he did it?"

"He doesn't share the details. Just 'They had it coming.' If you ask me, your team should be worried about the lack of a closer and a weak middle line-up, not that some old Indian chocked their wheels."

"The front office obsesses over a closer. But legends are funny things with ballplayers. Look at the Cubs. All those years, saddled to a goat."

"And you're here to pow-wow with the shaman. What, did you draw the short straw?"

Mathis glanced up as a spread of branches rushed past overhead. He decided a convertible would be far too distracting for him to drive. "I volunteered."

Raines chuckled. "You're an odd duck, Mathis."

Mathis didn't respond. He doubted Raines would get it. Mathis was a third-generation Cherokees fan. His family lived fifteen miles outside of Louisville. Some of his favorite memories were from the ballpark with his father and grandfather. There was never any thought of rooting for another team. The Cherokees were theirs, to celebrate or bemoan as necessary. Usually the latter.

When a job opened in the team's public affairs office,

Mathis jumped on it. There were more lucrative careers, more challenging roles, but Mathis wanted to be part of the Cherokee family, win or lose.

"Do *you* actually believe this curse thing?" Raines's question pierced Mathis's reverie.

"No. It has more to do with the idea of your grandfather. I think there's value in a psychological exorcism."

"What, no actors with Native American costumes in Louisville?"

"We want the players to know we tried to get as close as possible to the man who 'cursed' them. To be honest, I was surprised your grandfather was even alive."

"Good thing he is," Raines said. "My father passed when I was a boy, and I didn't go in for the shamanism. With me, you'd get a guy in a suit and a microphone, telling them the curse will be ended once they stop swinging at the first pitch."

Raines angled the car into a driveway leading to a blue and white striped trailer home.

"This is the place?" Mathis asked.

Raines nodded. "Batter up."

~o~

Victor Raincrow appeared every one of his hundred and three years. His features might have been carved from his flesh by unrelenting wind. Wrinkled canyons radiated in spokes from his eyes, twin pools of obsidian intimidation that showed the early clouds of cataracts. Parallel crags crossed his brow and dipped down to graze the bridge of his nose. His cheeks and chin were covered by lines, worn into a skin bronzed by over a century in the sun. All of it was capped by a full head of white hair, pulled tightly to the back in a pony tail.

Mathis made the team's pitch. In exchange for the ritual to lift the curse, the owner would make a public apology broadcast during the ESPN pre-game. The team would also set up a college scholarship fund for the Cherokee Nation in the amount of $50,000.

Raincrow sat on the edge of his rocking recliner as if it would swallow him should he lean back. "Piss on you, Baseball Man."

"Please tell me I haven't come all the way here just for that."

"You want more? Piss on your owner, your team, your stadium and your merchandising arm. And twice on your mascot. He dresses like a Navajo. A *Navajo*, you stupid sons of bitches. Hell, Louisville used to be Shawnee land. You can't even get being wrong right."

"Grandfather, you should consider their deal," Raines said. "They're offering a lot. It's an excellent opportunity to right the wrong."

"Right the wrong? You partied at Tulane on a full scholarship for four years. You liked it so much you went into the party industry. What do you know about wrongs?" Raincrow turned his attention back to Judge Judy on the old television. Mathis and Raines sat on the couch. It was upholstered in cowhide faded with age and frayed at the edges. The air was uncomfortable in the trailer, windows opened to an absence of breeze.

"Mister Raincrow," Mathis began, "I understand this is difficult–"

"I said piss on you, Baseball Man. Are you hard of hearing?" Raincrow glanced at his grandson. "I was embarrassed by these men, Roger. I should come to you in the form of a viper and bite you on the ass for bringing this crap into my home." He fixed his stare on Mathis. "How did you even find me?"

"We had a newspaper clipping in the team archive. Buried in the pages of the Louisville Times on July 28, 1931 was a note about Victor Raincrow, member of the Cherokee Nation, who was ejected during a game against the Pirates for causing a commotion in the grandstand. Once I had the name, I started searching the Internet. Led me right to you."

Raincrow snorted. "I should have bought that old fallout shelter to live in."

"The article mentioned how in retaliation for the ejection, you placed a curse on the team."

"Absolutely true."

"That was over eighty years ago."

"You can count something besides balls and strikes. The league must be proud."

"That's a long time to hold a grudge."

Raincrow stared at Mathis. Mathis felt weight in the gaze. A smile curled the old Cherokee's lips. "It is. So ask me why I did it, smart ass."

~o~

It was his twenty-second birthday, and Victor Raincrow had never seen a professional baseball game. He'd traveled to Louisville on tribal business with his cousin, Henry Blackfox. They were conveying four boxes of records to a man from the Bureau of Indian Affairs. Henry was used to the long trips from the reservation in the Ford pick-up, but it was the first time Victor had been to the city. The size of the buildings, the noise and hurry of cars and trolleys, the large numbers of people–all foreign to life on the reservation–kept Victor's head turning.

Having made the delivery to the bureau, Henry revealed he'd traded with someone in the office for two tickets, and asked his cousin if he wanted to see baseball. Victor agreed, beside himself with anticipation. The tribe had produced major leaguers–Ben Tincup, Jim Bluejacket, Zack Wheat. Victor and his friends considered them heroes. The boys spent summers scanning newspapers or hounding their fathers for news of Cherokee exploits in the major leagues. They played loosely organized games with improvised equipment in the dirt lot near the school, all-day affairs that left them exhausted, caked with grime from mingled dust and sweat.

Standing outside the Cherokees stadium, thinking of those childhood games, Victor was enthralled.

He followed Henry through the turnstile and tucked his ticket stub in his pocket. He walked among men in suits with cigars in their mouths and children with caps on their heads. They made their way to their seats, a dozen rows from the field. Victor could see players milling about the dugout, laughing at jokes he couldn't hear, stretching and warming up. The murmur of the crowd, the blue sky and sunlight above the curved walls of the stadium, the smells of grass and dirt all washed over Victor in amazing combination.

Then a section of the outfield wall opened and a half-dozen horses galloped onto the field, and the sky began to fall.

~o~

"They were marking the centennial of the *Nunna daul Isunyi*." Victor's voice was so heavy with disgust, his words should have clattered to the floor. "That's the Trail of Tears to you, Baseball Man. They were wrong by seven years–the Choctaw were the first tribe subjected to forced migration, in 1831. The Cherokee didn't get a turn in the bucket until 1838. Your team hired bare-chested day-laborers to play the braves, with hatchets in their hands and feathers in their hair. They rode washed-up race horses and whooped like they fell out of a Three Stooges short. These 'Cherokees' harassed settlers until they were escorted off by soldiers to 'new and prosperous homesteads,' according to the announcer. Like Andrew Jackson himself had civilized us. The crowd ate it up."

Mathis sighed, ashamed. "Mister Raincrow, I'm sorry."

"We've had language, government, and culture for centuries, and there I was, watching your organization peddling that savages-go-wild crap," Victor said. "I grew up listening to my grandfather tell us about the *Nunna daul Isunyi*, how he survived it while four thousand others didn't. But in your stadium, named for my people, the Cherokee was the villain. So I cursed the whole enterprise, from the buttons on their caps to the dirt in their spikes. All I needed was a little spit, and that's all baseball players do. I knew more about incantations by the time I was ten than you could read up on in a lifetime. I put a modified version of the *DIDA'LATLI''TĬ* on them. The incantation to destroy life. But I didn't destroy them. I just cut their balls off." He laughed, a brittle sound, and turned the television on again. Judge Judy had given way to an entertainment news program.

"Mister Raincrow, I'm not unfamiliar with the forced relocation. I have serious personal issues with the theft of your lands and your lives." Mathis felt naked. "I'm also not surprised by what my predecessors did. They were ignorant men in an unenlightened age, and their actions were inexcusable. All I can do is reassure you that we are not them." Mathis could see Victor, even while facing the television, was listening with rapt attention. "You've heard what my team has to offer, but I want to hear what you'd like us to do to restore our honor."

Victor turned. He squinted, trying to see if Mathis was shining him on. "I underestimated you, Baseball Man. Maybe you understand what side of the bread the butter goes on." He muted the television. "I've waited a long time for the Cherokees to send someone. I'm like that poor bastard DiMaggio, waiting for the Yankees to call him with a job offer after his final at-bat. I've pondered what I would ask if your team offered me something to end their suffering, what would help me let it go. There's really only one thing I want."

Mathis waited. "Yes?"

"Rename the team. Do that, and I'll lift the curse. Call them anything you want: the White Devils, the Dirty Jockstraps, I don't care."

"I would do it in a heartbeat, but I can't offer that. It's above my pay grade."

"Who can?"

"I presume that would be the owner's call."

"Tell him that's my price. Otherwise, the curse stays in place and your team can suck until the day after no one plays the game anymore."

~o~

"I won't do it," Paulson said.

Paulson was a short, narrow man, a fifty-something who looked ten years older. In his brown suit with his close crop of overly-dyed black hair, he looked like a stubbed-out cigar.

They sat at a table in the owner's suite overlooking the third base line. Below, the Cherokees were deadlocked with Atlanta in the eighth. "I'm not going to be a hostage to some geriatric Native American that wants to exploit superstitious nonsense. We'll hire an actor."

"If we do, Raincrow will discredit the entire event," Mathis said. "If the players think we tried to con them? We'll be even worse off than we were before." Mathis had been mulling Victor's story since leaving the man's trailer. Was Victor's request out of proportion to what had happened? It had been over eighty years; but Mathis hadn't been on the receiving end of the insult, or the events leading up to it.

He wasn't sure he wouldn't have done the same thing.

Paulson was overwound and about to spring apart. "Does he have any idea what it costs to rebrand a team? To conceive of an entirely new presentation and marketing strategy? Besides, he cursed us! I didn't even own the damned team when they did this show that bent him out of shape. Why doesn't he go after them?"

"I'm pretty sure that was the point of the curse." Mathis wondered what fates had befallen the owner and front office employees back in the day. Everyone remembered the careers of players. Did anyone know how people like the ticket takers and mail room clerks had fared?

"Curse. Pah. It's all in their heads. 'How did you miss that pop-up?' 'The curse got in my eyes.' I don't need the mumbo-jumbo of some old shaman. I need discipline. Confidence. Not excuses."

Before Mathis could reply, the meager crowd in the stadium produced a flurry of boos and catcalls. Paulson shouted to Alan Phipps, the team's head of baseball operations, who was watching the game from the seats outside the suite, overlooking the field. "What happened?"

"We lost the lead. Now we're in the middle of a fist-fight. Taylor called for a pitch out. Pagliano tried, but the ball took a crazy turn in and hit the batter's bat. It dribbled down the first base line. Fair ball, runner scored from third, and Taylor's throw to first was late. Braves are on top."

"If Pagliano didn't hit the batter, what started the fight?"

Phipps was lost between bemusement and despair. "It's a family affair. Taylor is trying to punch Pagliano's lights out. I need to check the media guide, but I think this is a first."

Paulson turned back to Mathis. Events bowed his brow. "So what are we calling this shaman shindig?"

~o~

The Friday evening after the All-Star break, the Louisville Cherokees hosted the "Cherokees Public Restoration Event" from a platform erected at home plate. It wasn't a sellout crowd, despite the advertising, but Mathis saw victory in moving 30,000 tickets in a season where 10,000 was a gate-buster.

Paulson didn't look much better in his blue suit than

his brown. He opened with a public acknowledgment and condemnation of the events surrounding Victor's ejection. He apologized for the insensitive and ignorant acts that had driven the shaman to curse the team. He offered as conciliation a promise to the Cherokee Nation: Paulson would rename the team after the season was over as a symbol of respect for the Cherokee people, and in appreciation of Victor's mercy.

Victor emerged from the tunnel behind the plate in a ceremonial headdress and robes. He began to chant, dancing in smooth, tight circles beside the platform. His head bobbed with such fervor, Mathis expected the headdress to fly apart. He couldn't believe the man was over a century old.

Victor's colored robes flowed on the light breeze as he danced down the first base line. His chant was broadcast throughout the stadium via wireless lavaliere microphone. Victor seemed to draw energy from the crowd. A cheer started as the shaman made his way around the field. It grew louder as he progressed, each section on its feet as he passed, the ceremony taken in and processed and fed back to him.

Mathis studied the Cherokees players, lined up outside the dugout. The expressions on their faces were a mix of amusement, curiosity, wonder–hope?

It took ten minutes for Victor to circle the field. By the time he crossed the plate to complete his circuit, the crowd was in a frenzy. A hush fell when Victor stopped chanting. He ascended the platform and stood before Paulson. He stared at the owner and stepped to the microphone. The shaman didn't even appear winded.

"The honor of the Cherokee Nation has been restored," Victor said. The crowd went nuts. Despite the adulation directed at him, his tone was grim. "In accordance with our terms, my curse upon your tribe is lifted."

Paulson clapped Victor on the back and shook his hand. Mathis thought Victor was going to slug the owner. Cameras around the park gave firefly flashes that continued as the pair descended the platform. The old shaman walked beside Paulson, his face neutral. When they reached the entrance to the backstop tunnel, Victor stopped and leaned over to Mathis. His whisper was quick, harsh.

"If you cross me, I'll make the first curse look like a Disney cruise." He spat a clot of phlegm into the dust at Mathis's feet for emphasis. "Count on it."

Mathis nodded. He watched the shaman walk down the tunnel to his dressing room.

That night, the Cherokees lost a squeaker to the Diamondbacks on a blown call at the plate, 7-6. Cherokees Manager Andre Mostell quipped at the post-game press conference the new curse was apparently the umpires' vision plan.

~o~

On August 1, the Cherokees were 16 games behind the Central Division leading Cardinals. The visit by the shaman to their ballpark two weeks earlier was being dismissed as a failed publicity stunt.

On August 15, the Cherokees were 10 games behind the Cardinals. Words such as "rejuvenated" and "streaking" were used by sportswriters in Louisville. In Saint Louis, the terms "ice-cold" and "slumping" were bandied about.

On September 1, the Cherokees weren't knocking on the door of the Central Division lead. They were kicking it in with twenty-six pairs of cleats.

On September 15, the Cherokees took the lead in the division for the first time since Opening Day, 1994. People used the shaman as a lead-in to other discussions, but Mathis could tell Victor was on their minds.

Mathis spent the summer watching the Cherokees ascend, unable to fully enjoy it. Raines dialed him as if they were college buddies. He asked questions about the renaming. He made suggestions about players and the line-up. He sniffed around for insider information. Every call made Mathis feel like Raines was trying to create a role for himself with the team. Mathis began to wonder if he'd need an exorcist next.

When Raines wasn't hammering Mathis, Paulson was driving him crazy. "I don't know how I was bullied into this," became the closing line to every conversation. Paulson's new position in the spotlight caused him anxiety. He made tentative decisions for the team's new direction, then reversed course when the press weighed in on them. He grew tight-lipped. Plans came from his office in old faucet drips. The stock comment to the media, to fans, to everyone became a cryptic, "we'll have more information soon."

It sounded legitimate in July. By September, it took on the patina of stalling.

~o~

The Cherokees played for the top slot in the National League Central division on the last Sunday of the season. They had clinched the wild card playoff slot two nights earlier. They were guaranteed a postseason for the first time since the Hoover administration. Mathis felt greedy for wanting more.

He watched the final game of the season from his apartment with a stack of folders and a couple of beers. He'd had seats at the park, but had gifted them to a friend. Between postseason preparations and the team's efforts toward rebranding, Mathis was buried in work.

The evening the Cherokees clinched the wild card, Paulson assembled a brand transition team and handed out what he called "exploratory tasks." Mathis was on the hook for developing a preliminary list of new names and mascots for a naming contest. He'd come up with a dozen. Mathis was partial to the Mockingbirds. The idea of rivalry games between the Cardinals and Mockingbirds appealed to him.

The Lions and the Chickadees were also early favorites. In some corners, the Sluggers was proving popular, but Mathis had no desire to swap one naming nightmare for another.

Pagliano was throwing his sixth gem in a row. He'd been reborn in the second half. His delivery was smooth, the ball lively. The Cherokees plated five runs early to support his shutout effort. The team hummed, a batting and throwing machine that ground the Reds beneath its wheels.

Mathis held his breath through the final out, a mundane pop-up to third. He'd seen enough mundane pop-ups go wrong in his life. This time, Foster Curtis squeezed it tight to close the door. The fans, fair-weather and unashamed, spilled onto the field in celebration, and the police were loathe to restrain them. Mathis watched the spectacle with a child's grin and long draws on his beer.

The TV crew was already in the clubhouse when the players arrived. Mathis watched a room awash in champagne and post-game interviews. Pagliano, who collected the complete game win, was unaccustomed to praise and humble with the reporter. He gave way to Andre Mostell and William Paulson.

The third question from the reporter went to Paulson. "Now that the Cherokees have won the division, do you intend to keep the promise you made to the Cherokee shaman who lifted his curse?"

The owner paused. Mathis realized he was holding his breath again. He saw a flicker of doubt on Paulson's face. The length of a heartbeat felt to Mathis like cardiac arrest.

"The Cherokee baseball organization is honorable," Paulson said, "and Victor Raincrow kept his word. We're anxious to put the past behind us. Tomorrow morning, we will be holding a press conference to announce full details about the renaming of the team for next season, including our timeline and some ways the public will be asked to contribute."

Mathis exhaled.

The reporter persisted. "What can you share about a new team name?"

Paulson nodded. "We're planning a naming contest for this December, but I don't know. With a season like this, maybe we should just call ourselves the Louisville Miracles."

"You'll probably have me fix the contest," Mathis muttered. Paulson had insisted the Miracles move directly to the short list.

Mathis sat back and finished his beer. He picked up his cell phone to call his father. A typical season ended with a postmortem barbecue at his father's house with family and associated hangers-on. For once, Mathis felt like taking everyone out to celebrate.

Before he could dial out, the phone rang. Raines. Mathis thought about sending it to voicemail, answered instead. "Roger! I don't know if you saw, but Paulson's just announced a press conference for tomorrow morning, with all the detail you could want about our brand-new identity. They're loving your grandfather in Louisville tonight. Except the Cherokee Scout. He's probably at the tavern across the street from the stadium drowning his sorrows, provided he can get the head of that stupid costume unfastened."

"My grandfather died about an hour ago," Raines said.

"Jesus. I'm sorry. What happened?"

"We were on the sixth hole at the Funplex yesterday. He had a massive heart attack."

Mathis frowned. "Roger, I'm sorry. That's horrible. I wish I'd gotten to thank him for everything. I really don't think we'd have gotten here without him. I'll talk to Paulson. I'm going to make sure they have a moment of silence for Victor before the first game of the Division series."

"You might want to wait on that."

Something in the man's tone gave Mathis a chill. "What do you mean?"

"My grandfather was so bitter and so angry for so long,

you know? He liked you, Baseball Man, he did. In his way. But your owner dragged it out, and my grandfather was certain your team was going to screw him. Especially if he died before the season was done." Roger sighed. "He put the curse back. With his dying breath. Unconditional, unapologetic, irrevocable. Dialed to eleven." Raines had the somber calm of a funeral director. "I'm sorry. If you guys had given him a little reassurance along the way–"

"What does that mean, you're sorry? We're changing the name. The legal wheels are in motion. I'm holding a list of new mascots in my hand. Mockingbirds, Roger! I have mockingbirds!"

"The best suggestion I have is to get out of there before it takes hold."

"Get out? This is my team. It's always been my team. And we were all on the same team, all of us, and look what we did together! Everybody got what they wanted! Now you're telling me he just... put it back?"

"I really am sorry. You guys did right by him in the end. It's not your fault he got twitchy. It's not fair." Then Raines added, almost an afterthought, "Good luck."

The line disconnected. Mathis stared at his cell phone. He was still trying to figure out what he was going to tell Paulson when behind him on the broadcast, he heard the ESPN reporter say something about Pagliano catching a champagne cork in the eye.

–o–

SHADY ACRES

THE LAKE WAS AS quiet as Roger remembered. He hadn't been there in a dozen years, but the mirrored finish of still waters and the light hum of the first spring insects reminded him why he liked the spot. Ringed pines encircled it like children holding hands. It was nestled in the mountains, secluded at the end of three miles of still-thawing trail. They'd find the car in the parking lot, but his footprints would be gone with the next rain. There'd be plenty of that as spring gained momentum.

He sat beside a flat rock in the soft ground, sank a little. His seat was damp and he found it didn't matter. He tugged the folded slip of paper from his pocket, opened it along the creases, read it for the hundredth time. The words never changed. Inch wide mass, bulls-eye just left of center, tucked between the Thalamus and the Corpus Callosum, as if neatly put away by the maid. Five hundred words on wasting, slow degradation, loss of motor skill and memory and self were summed up in a single, final pronouncement: inoperable.

Roger refolded the page and put it back in the jacket pocket, beside his wallet. He'd written a letter to his sister and posted it on his way out of town. She was the most responsible person left to him, and while his decision would hurt her, she would also see to taking care of him. He was phobic about losing the things that made him who he was. There would be no protracted suffering for the people around him, or for himself.

It was a suitable weapon–Smith & Wesson .357, dark as death and heavy in his hand. Fresh from the pawn shop, it stunk of gun oil and a promise. Roger hefted it in his hand, listening to the birds until he reached his point of strongest resolve. He hedged his bets with a prayer. He palmed the grip, thumbed off the safety, cocked the hammer, pressed the barrel under his chin.

Something moved in the corner of his eye as he squeezed the trigger, a distraction–

Thunder. Light. Pain. Heaven conspicuously like a tree-ringed lake. Sideways. *Pain*.

Spasming arm stirring dead leaves. Gun in the dirt. Out of reach. *Pain*.

Rustling. By the lake. Something coming. Grizzly bear. Skinny. *Pain*.

Up from hibernation.

Sniffing.

Hungry.

–o–

Erin Beiber's Wild Ride

The ride was old, battered. Jimmy surmised it had been assembled and disassembled a thousand times before stopping in the Jamesway parking lot.

"No way," he told Peter. "It's a deathtrap."

As if to punctuate the point, the six-car train rattled past them on a downhill, stirring the humid air. The roller coaster drowned out the cacophony of the midway–the crowd and barkers and music from the carnival's other rides–that filled the Saturday night.

"Wuss," Peter declared, and the pack of boys with him–a pack with which Jimmy didn't run–followed his lead.

"Baby."

"Ginny."

"He'd probably cry like a girl."

Jimmy shrugged. "I heard three kids were killed last year over in Pinesville when the Flying Bobs came loose."

"I heard you piss your bed," Peter said, and threw an unwelcome arm around Erin Beiber. Erin had been standing beside the line talking to friends, blue eyes and braces framed by her summer-bleached hair. Her sun dress announced her victory in the race to puberty. Peter had already allowed a couple groups to pass in line so he could linger near Erin, alternating glances between her eyes and her budding curves.

Erin shoved him hard in the chest. "Don't touch me, creep." She stepped away. Jimmy caught the anger in Peter's eyes.

"Bitch," Peter muttered. "C'mon. Ginny can stay here with the other girls."

The pack laughed as they formed up their line at the roller coaster–the Python, according to the sign in front with a dozen bulbs burned out.

Jimmy heard Erin behind him. "They've made a terrible mistake."

Jimmy turned and saw her staring at the ride, her eyes glassy. The air around them became thicker. Jimmy thought if he touched her, they'd arc electricity. "What do you mean?"

"Sometimes I see things in my dreams. On Monday I saw him," she pointed to the guy running the Python, a thirty-something carny in a Phish t-shirt, "when they were setting up. His wife called and asked him for a divorce. He got distracted."

Peter and the others whooped as they boarded the coaster. The carny restrained them, returned to the console, and pressed a button. The chain caught the bottom of the string of cars and began dragging it up the first hill. Erin continued through the clanking. She might have been narrating a film strip.

"The bolts at the bottom of the first drop are too tight. On the next run, the torque from the train will finally sheer them off. The track will separate. The cars will jump the rails and crash into the framework. Ricky, Barry and John will break some bones. Tony will lose his left arm. Kevin will be crushed. Peter will be decapitated by the beam."

The cars crested the hill, rounded a curve, pitched forward into the first drop. Jimmy watched them plummet, man-sized bullets. He heard the shouts of excitement.

A metallic grunt punched through it all. Jimmy turned away as the first car sailed from the track. The screams of excitement were silenced by the shriek of twisting steel and an unnatural thunder, replaced by different cries of terror.

People rushed past Jimmy and Erin. He watched her staring at the carnage he couldn't face. A siren rose in the distance.

"You said you saw this on Monday." Jimmy's heart was a kettle drum beneath his ribs. "Why didn't you tell anyone?"

Erin exhaled. She'd been holding her breath. "One night last month, I saw Peter when he was sixteen. He and two other boys forced me to do things. Horrible things. With them." She turned her cold gaze on Jimmy, and he understood what she meant. "Who would have believed me? This is better. Don't you see?"

She began to walk away through the swirling crush of onlookers stretching for a glimpse of the Python. Jimmy's stomach churned. He shivered through his sweat, called after her. "Erin? Have you ever dreamt about me?"

She turned back. Her expression was weighted with an unfathomable pity, a beguiling absence of joy. Then she was swallowed by the chaos of the crowd.

–o–

THE TRAPDOOR

THEY'D BEEN IN THE house six months when Jude decided she wanted to pull the carpets and restore the hardwood.

"When it freezes, you're going to feel it," Darryl told her. The place was a pier and beam bungalow, a kit house. Seventy years old, its underside was open to airflow year-round.

"You can buy me slippers for Christmas." She took his glass, walked to the kitchen, topped off their wine and returned, snuggling in next to him. "Besides, hardwood is hot right now. It'll add value to this place when it comes time to sell."

He knew she had no interest in flipping the house. She'd wanted something more suburban than the condo, someplace to put roots and build a family. It had been a couple of years since the miscarriage, and Darryl saw evidence of her desire to nest, despite Jude's insistence the second bedroom was intended for guests.

His mind lingered on the miscarriage, and Darryl pushed

the memory deeper inside, guilt tearing him like a swallowed fishhook. "I don't know the first thing about stripping floors."

"You don't need to. You'll be at work for most of it anyway. It'll keep you from getting underfoot." She poked the sole of his bare foot and he squirmed. "But you can help me move furniture and pull up this ugly carpeting."

It *was* ugly. Worn on the edges, with an odd mix of colors and geometric patterns, it reminded Darryl of something salvaged from an old hotel two steps ahead of the wrecking ball. Staring at it gave him a mild headache.

"That'll be a pleasure," he said.

~o~

They found the trapdoor in the center of the living room floor.

It was flush with the floorboards, two feet square, built from a series of angular, interlocking pieces of different-colored woods. The design reminded Darryl of a pinwheel. A ring handle of black iron was set in a notch on one side. In the center of the ring was a keyhole. Darryl didn't see any hinges.

"Why would anyone put a door here?" Jude asked. She knelt beside it.

"Maintenance access, probably. Easier than shimmying all the way under the house." Darryl hooked a finger through the handle, pulled, pushed. The trapdoor was locked. "Not very useful if you can't open it."

"Maybe that's why they covered it." Jude traced the inlays with her slender fingers. "The design is nice. Someone put a lot of work into it, considering what it is. It's almost a shame to stain over it."

"We don't have to decide anything right now."

"Ow!" Jude jerked her hand away. A drop of blood splattered one of the inlays.

"What happened?"

122

"I must have caught an edge." She sucked on her fingertip, then studied it. "Damn, that's deep."

She held it out to Darryl. He didn't see a splinter. There was a gouge where the skin had been torn. He watched the blood pool in the wound. Another drop ran down the side of her finger and fell to the floor.

"That's not how we want to stain the wood," Darryl said, and grabbed a tissue from the box on the side table. He wrapped it around the fingertip. "Let's get that cleaned out."

Jude studied the seam where her finger had caught. Darryl saw her frown. She blotted the blood spots on the inlay with the tissue around her finger.

"Weird," she said. "It looked so smooth."

He laid awake in the dark, cataloging the sounds of the night. Jude snored beside him. It varied from a light, wheezy breath to the occasional thirty second burst of buzz-saw intensity. The refrigerator compressor clicked on and hummed twice an hour in the kitchen. Beyond the walls, the whistles of freight locomotives in the distance split the night.

He laid awake and thought about how he'd poisoned Jude.

No, not Jude. The baby. Clifford's baby.

Clifford was the muscle-head that lived upstairs in the condo building, with the bright blue eyes and the best smile money could buy. He was always there with compliments for Jude and digs at Darryl, asides about how he could tone this or tighten that. Darryl wasn't in bad shape. He was a few pounds heavy. Clifford made ten sound like fifty.

Darryl didn't realize Jude and Clifford were getting together. He was wrapped up in work, missing her signals, adrift from her. He did notice she was more quiet, giving him space. He presumed it was because work had made him prickly.

He discovered Jude was pregnant from the discarded test. He might not have found it if the garbage bag hadn't snagged on the bent corner of the chute and torn open. The plastic stick jutted from the pile of debris that landed on the floor, a plus sign with a dozen secrets.

He knew the baby wasn't his. He'd cut his share of health classes in school, but the requisite precursor hadn't occurred with Jude for at least four months.

After finding the test, he spent the next few days watching, paying attention, waiting for Jude to tell him something. Instead, she flowed back into the space she'd created, engaged with him, seemed recommitted to him. He could tell whatever had been going on had ended. It wasn't until he realized Clifford couldn't meet his eye any longer and his digs had turned to silence that Darryl put it together.

Then Jude began musing aloud about children. Were they ready? Did a child fit in their lives? Could they manage?

"Is there something you want to tell me?" he asked after one such round of contemplation over dinner.

Jude shook her head and shrugged it off. "Just thinking out loud."

It was then Darryl decided he didn't want Clifford's legacy determining the course of his life with Jude. He still wanted her. He didn't want the baby she was dancing around.

A propeller plane droned past overhead. The dog up the street barked at the wind. Beside Darryl, Jude rolled in her sleep and draped an arm over him. He caressed it and closed his eyes. He wondered if the buzz in his head was the sound of self-loathing.

~o~

That Saturday morning, Jude woke him with a shake and an excited smile. "I found the key!"

Half-awake, Darryl had no idea what she was talking

about. He hadn't given the trapdoor much thought. He looked up at the object she dangled above him, a shaped piece of metal the same color as the trapdoor's lock and handle. It was on a piece of dirty twine.

"Huh. Where was it?"

"On top of one of the kitchen cabinets," she said. "The one by the sink has a recessed top. I was putting up your old Warner Brothers glasses. It was in the dust."

Darryl propped himself on one elbow. "Have you tried it?

"Yes. It's unlocked, but it won't budge. I'm thinking it might have been nailed closed outside, or it's rusted shut." She gave him a coy grin. "I was wondering if you wanted to take a trip under the house after breakfast."

~o~

He could hear the *tap tap tap* of the broom handle on the floor boards. He'd told Jude to signal in intervals so he could find the right spot as he worked his way under the house on his back. He picked the path that had the fewest obstacles–low-hanging pipes and discarded bricks or stones–but there still wasn't a direct line to the underside of the living room. Darryl shimmied around piers and under plumbing until he was positioned beneath the sound.

"Can you hear me?" he asked. Above him, Jude tapped once on the floor for yes. Darryl shined the beam of his small flashlight on the bottom of the house.

He didn't see any sign of a trapdoor.

Even if the underside was plain wood instead of the ornate inlays displayed on the top side of the panel, the same seams would have been visible. There should have been hinges, at least. "Honey, am I in the right spot?"

There was another single rap of the broom handle on the floor above Darryl. Then there was a metallic thud and something struck Darryl in the face.

~o~

A peal of thunder woke him. He opened his eyes to darkness.

The night air was damp. He could hear rain rattling the gutters. Darryl's back ached from laying on the uneven ground. He could hear Jude somewhere above him, inside the house, sobbing.

"Baby?" he called. Jude didn't answer.

Darryl worked his way back to the edge of the house, his head throbbing. Had the trapdoor come unstuck and hit him? If so, why had Jude left him under the house all day?

He slid from beneath the dwelling and laid on his back in the wet grass and falling rain. He felt his forehead. There was a lump, painful to the touch and tacky with blood from a gash he couldn't see. He stood and fought off a wave of nausea.

He entered through the back door and made his way through the kitchen and dining room. He turned the corner into the living room. All the lights were on. Jude was huddled in the far corner. Her knees were pulled up to her chin. Her eyes were red and swollen from crying. She didn't seem to see Darryl.

"Jude? What happened?"

Jude was somewhere else. She sobbed, eyes fixed on the trapdoor. Darryl crossed the room, knelt beside her.

"Jude, look at me."

He touched her arm. She recoiled and screamed. She turned her gaze on him. The scream stopped. She gasped. Then she hugged him as if her life depended on not letting go.

~o~

"It opened," she said later, when she'd calmed. They sat on the bed. He'd brought her a beer, but she hadn't taken more than a sip.

"I know." Darryl pushed the hair on his forehead to

126

display the gash. Cleaned up, it felt worse than it appeared. He was still debating whether he should have it x-rayed for a fracture. "Why didn't you check on me after it hit me?"

She shook her head. "You weren't there."

"I sure as hell didn't go anywhere, being unconscious and all."

Jude had stopped crying, but her body seemed compelled to the fetal position. "No, I mean you weren't wherever the trapdoor opened into."

Darryl stared at her. "It's a door in the floor. It goes to the outside."

"No it doesn't. It opens somewhere else. To steps that go down."

"There are no steps under there," Darryl said. "There's no room for them. It's eighteen inches high. Stairs couldn't go anywhere even if–"

"You're not hearing me. The trapdoor doesn't go under the house. It goes somewhere else. There are stairs that lead down in a spiral."

"That's physically impossible."

"Oh, it's possible. It's very fucking possible."

"Did you go down these steps?"

"No," she said, and paused. "He came up."

Darryl studied her. She'd been in shock when he came inside. Now she was collected and alert, but what she was saying was bat-shit crazy. "*Who* came up?"

Her gaze was hard. "The baby." She swallowed. "The baby that you killed. That *we* killed."

Darryl's heart skipped. He opened his mouth, but nothing came out.

"He knew all about it," Jude continued. "How you poisoned me. He knew about the celandine and feverfew you mixed into my food to encourage the miscarriage." Darryl saw a sheen of tears build in her eyes. "He told me he knew I let you."

"You *what*?" It came out despite his dry tongue and lips. He'd done his homework when he'd decided he didn't want her to have the baby. There were a number of herbs that would encourage a body to miscarry. Very simple, very natural, readily available from the health food store up the street from the condo. He'd wanted it to seem an accident.

She nodded. "You think I didn't know about your hiding places? I was looking for money to visit a doctor. I wasn't stupid. I knew if I was knocked up, it was Cliff's. I was terrified. Cliff wanted no part of it. And after I felt you out, I thought if I told you, you'd leave." She sniffled and he thought she might cry again. "I found the bottles. In a way, I was relieved you figured out on your own." A frown creased her lips. "I presume you found the pregnancy test."

Darryl nodded. He felt like he was falling.

"I did some reading when I found the herbs. I realized what you were doing. At first, I thought your method of dealing with it was fucked up. But the more I thought about it, the more it felt like the perfect solution. It let us both live with the lie. It let us stay together. And it let me off the hook. For a while."

Darryl took a deep breath, exhaled. "I'm sorry."

"So am I. Because now we need to care for him."

"What are you talking about?"

"He lives in the twilight between worlds. We destroyed him, and now we have to atone. That's why he made the door here in the floor. Why he came through it. To tell me that we needed to go to him. He was our blessing. We were selfish and we murdered him, and now he's our curse."

"Jude, this isn't possible. You've had a shock. You've imagined something."

"He's coming back in three days." She stood from the bed, walked into the bathroom. "For both of us."

She closed the bathroom door behind her.

He picked up the phone and dialed 911.

128

~o~

"Is she going to be okay?"

Darryl looked across the desk at Mikey, his boss. He'd had to tell Mikey about Jude being hospitalized. He'd concocted a story to cover the gash in the forehead–*Oh, that. Got dizzy getting out of the tub, fell and whacked it on the sink*–and omitted the rest.

"They're going to keep her a few days for observation. They think it's some kind of stress response to the anniversary of the miscarriage." Jude had repeated continuously as they wheeled her through the hospital that her baby was returning in three days. The doctor had her on a mild sedative and had kept her for tests.

"Take the time you need," Mikey said. Darryl figured Mikey was already wondering if Jude had bashed him with a lamp or something.

Darryl traveled from work to the hospital to the house the first two nights. He held her hand and talked to her, but Jude didn't notice he was in the room. She muttered unintelligible words and stared at the ceiling. At night, back in their bed, Darryl was one with the darkness and tried to ignore sounds he didn't recognize.

When Darryl arrived to see her on the third evening, the nurses were frantic. Jude was missing. She'd gotten dressed and simply walked out of the ward, then the hospital. The only person with whom she'd spoken on her way out was Mrs. Glennon, an elderly woman in the room two doors down who was hooked to an IV and clutching a walker when Darryl spoke with her.

"Oh, yes," Mrs. Glennon volunteered. "I saw her. Such a nice girl. She was talking about going to see her baby."

~o~

The front door was open wide in the sweep of Darryl's headlights. He parked in the street and ran to the house. He flipped the switch inside the door. Light filled the room.

The trapdoor was open. The doorway yawned in the floor. A figure in a hooded gray robe stood beside the opening, leaning over it, peering down.

"Jude?" Darryl asked.

The figure in the robe turned towards him. Where Jude's face should have been visible under the hood, there was a deep, dark emptiness. On a woven cord around the figure's neck hung a life-sized face that might have been sculpted from alabaster. It was Jude's face, eyes wide with terror, mouth open in a silent scream.

Darryl heard a scratching sound from the opening. Small hands gripped the edge of the floorboards. A second figure climbed into view. This one was thin, naked. Its skin was sallow, its hair fine. Its genitalia declared it a boy. It appeared to be a couple years old, yet its blue eyes had an intelligence that transcended age.

It took Jude's hand and guided her to the opening. Darryl watched his wife disappear, slowly turning as she spiraled down the staircase. As she descended from view, Darryl stepped closer to the opening. There was light coming from below. He saw the top of the impossible staircase. He heard the murmur of distant voices, a garble of sounds that made him uneasy. Jude was gone.

The child moved between him and the opening. A sound rose, not in Darryl's ears but within his head, a wail that coalesced into a voice.

You must come too.

"Come where?" Darryl felt an itch, rubbed his nose. His fingertips came away stained with blood.

The boy ignored him. *But first, your mask.*

The wail rose again. Darryl felt as if someone was squeezing his head in a vise. His face stretched, shredded. He opened his eyes long enough against the pain to realize he could no longer see. He began to scream. Then his mouth was filled with blood and the scream became a terrible gagging.

The boy cooed. *Testify.*

Darryl saw himself through the child's eyes. His face was a churning pulp, skin fraying and muscles splitting against bone. His skull pushed forward, out from the bloody mass, but instead of eye sockets and teeth, it had his features. Darryl recognized the cold gaze, the haunted expression. It was the face he'd seen in the mirror the night he'd given Jude the dose that had finally pushed her body into the miscarriage.

His clothes transformed, rewove into the same robe Jude was wearing. The hood formed around the destroyed flesh of his face, the pulpy mass consumed by the void within, the ruin of who he was sinking into a sea of pitch.

The face of bone with its sorrowful expression hovered in the air. A cord slipped from the fabric of the robe, threaded through the back of the face and connected in a loop behind his neck. The face fell against his chest. He felt the sensation at the same time. When it struck him, as if watching a movie, his perspective changed from the boy's view to the eyes of the face strung around his neck.

Now your shame has no mask.

Darryl's heart thudded. The boy took his hand. The flesh was cold. He wanted to run, but his feet ignored him and took him instead to the trapdoor. Murmurs filtered up from the silvery light at the bottom of the staircase. There was a scream somewhere in the distance, terrified, forlorn. He wondered if it was Jude.

Where are we going? Darryl thought as he took the first step down. *Where does this lead?*

Behind him, the boy answered in a voice of grim joy.

Home. Daddy.

–o–

Tacklesmooches

TWO OF THEM HELD Joey's shoulders while Donnie, hand on the back of Joey's head, pressed his face half into the water, half against the porcelain. One of them slapped the handle.

Joey struggled against his disadvantage, failed. He was glad it was only the pink puck in his face, that one of them hadn't primed the urinal with piss on a whim before deciding to 'baptize' him. They'd tried that before. The arrival of Mister Martin, the custodian, had derailed their plan that time.

The roar of the flush faded, the urinal reinvented as the world's worst seashell. Three sets of hands yanked him backwards. Donnie punched him once in the stomach before they pitched him to the tile.

"Are you gonna talk about Claire again? Are you, you little jagoff?"

Denial was only going to get him kicked, and he wasn't willing to learn at the toe of a boot if Donnie would get away with it. Joey shook his head. "No. Not ever." Joey hadn't said anything about Claire. That was the hell of it.

He hated himself for caving in. He wasn't afraid to scrap, even though Donnie had six inches and forty pounds on him. He'd gone swing for swing with bigger, meaner, smarter than Donnie. His mother stayed his hand. She had enough to worry her since his father's open-ended trip to the corner for smokes: losing her job, getting evicted, having to come live with Aunt Sarah. Joey got in new-kid trouble at school, hated the cast of his mother's eyes when she retrieved him from the principal's office, the sad glance that felt like pity he couldn't avoid trouble, with a glimmer of guilt as if she'd somehow failed him.

To Joey, giving in to the Donnies of the world tasted like soot. Uncle Bernie called it "taking one for the team."

Donnie smiled at Joey, but it was something he hadn't mastered. One corner of his mouth pulled higher than the other, a misshapen rictus. "Tomorrow, jagoff." Equal parts threat and promise, the same refrain every day. Whether Claire had a pot to stir, or Donnie needed to scratch his sociopathic itch, tomorrow always happened: wedgies, getting shoved in the mud, books knocked from his hands, lunch money pilfered, things vanishing from his locker. Donnie was hip to limiting Joey's scars to psychological ones, with the occasional gut punch or nut-buster to shore up the intimidation.

It didn't help that Donnie's aunt, Miss Kiefer, was the hall and recess monitor. Joey'd tried to appeal to the woman before he knew who all the players were. She was aghast. Not *her* nephew. He'd *never* do such things. Joey knew then he was on his own until Donnie screwed up, broke an arm or made him piss blood.

Donnie and his thugs left Joey prone on the tile. The door swung closed, hinges crying out for oiling. Joey laid there, thankful for a minute–even prone on bathroom tile–where he wasn't looking over his shoulder, waiting for a hammer-blow.

He stood, gathered himself, pulled some folded paper towels from the dented metal dispenser, and dried what he could of himself and his clothes. He studied his face in the broad bathroom mirror. The oldest ten year old on earth stared back at him.

Moving in with Aunt Sara and Uncle Bernie made Joey a mid-year transfer, dropped into his class well after alliances had been won and friendships forged. He was short for his age. He wore glasses and the part in his hair was crooked. He was husky, not fat like Nelson the Belly in the fourth grade, but still above average, over-indulgence exacerbated by too much TV. He was a ready-made target for the boys in Mrs. Bolan's sixth grade class and their zero-tolerance policy for strays. Once they understood they could get a rise out of him, it was over. The guys in class did the things guys did when they perceived a weak dog in the pack. You got that with boys, whether you were tough or not. But the girls baffled him with their cruelty, trying to outdo each other's taunts and jokes at his expense. Claire's mission seemed to be humiliating him.

In his second week at school, Claire made a public show of inviting Joey to a party at her house. She said she wanted to make up for treating him badly since his arrival. Her friends agreed, spoke in kind tones with him, urged him to attend. They worked on him until he took the bait. When he arrived at the appointed place and time, there was no party. The elderly couple behind the door didn't understand why a young boy they didn't know was on their stoop, asking for a girl they'd never met. He discovered later she lived on the other side of town from where she'd directed him.

The rest followed Claire's lead with their own variations. Jeannie whipping his gym shorts down in front of the class was still the worst, but each took her shots.

Joey wanted out. No one had consulted him about moving into Aunt Sarah's house, hours away from Marty and Kevin and Kevin's dog, or the field where they wasted entire summers playing baseball with the other kids in the neighborhood. He'd been given no opinion about sleeping in the room off the kitchen that was too hot when the stove was on and smelled of old people gone and already forgotten.

The door screeched open and one of the hall monitors stepped inside. Joey didn't know the kid's name. He couldn't have been out of the third grade. "Bell's about to ring. You need to go back to class."

Joey dreaded the derisive snickers awaiting him. He wondered if the monitor would swap places.

~o~

Joey was usually safe at the end of the day, waiting for the bus. Donnie rode the Route 7 bus. It boarded on the other side of the playground, and you weren't allowed to stray from your bus lines. Joey didn't know which kids Donnie tortured before getting on the bus and returning to a neighborhood where Joey suspected pets went missing and windows were mysteriously broken in the dead of night. Only one of Donnie's crew rode the Route 3 bus, a dim bulb named Ralph. Ralph was a follower, absent the spark to take people on himself. He ignored Joey as a matter of principle.

Joey rode the bus with another outcast, a tall, skinny kid named Paulie. Paulie was cool. Paulie sat in the other half of the sixth grade, but they shared English and History class and watched each other's backs when they could. Paulie treated Joey like a brother. They talked about books. Paulie had read almost as many as Joey had, and he knew everything from the Hardy Boys right up to the more advanced stuff they were reading in junior high school.

Paulie glanced across the lot at Donnie as Joey relayed the day's events. Paulie was lanky. He came from tall parents. He didn't look like he could survive a stiff wind. He watched people like he was making mental lists. The depth of his

136

gaze suggested he was biding time until puberty arrived and reshuffled the deck.

"One of these days, I'm gonna pop him one," Joey puffed up. "Then they'll see he's not so tough."

"That only happens in the movies," Paulie said. "They'd still flatten you. Or at least warm you up for him."

While they talked, Claire marched up the crooked row of book bags. She rode the Route 5 bus, her line adjacent enough to fraternize with Joey's. There was no escaping her. Her face was framed in wavy hair so blond, it was white in the sunlight. She'd have been cute if not for the mocking eyes.

Joey saw her coming. Gave her his back. "Go away, Claire."

Claire huffed. "What's your issue?"

"If you have to ask, you're not as smart as you think."

"Do I have to tell Donnie you're talking trash about me again?"

Paulie had three sisters. He feared no girl. "We don't talk trash, we burn it. And with all that hairspray, you'd go up like a torch."

Claire's eyes went saucer. "You don't–you–" she sputtered out, returned to her line with an indignant stomp and waited for her bus with the clutch of girlfriends who'd been watching.

"One of us is going to pay for that," Joey said.

Paulie grinned, a toothy scarecrow. "Both of us, probably. But man, that felt good."

The Route 3 bus, lumbering and wheezing as if the school was perched on a summit in the Andes, rounded the corner at the end of Oak Street. Joey knew it by sound, a dog with a cough. He gathered his bag as the bus stopped for a light at a cross street. He happened to glance over at the grass that bordered the far end of the playground.

Joey saw a girl.

The first thing he noticed about her was the book in her hands. He recognized the cover. His copy of THE HOBBIT had the same one. She was walking in the grass, reading, weaving like a ribbon around the bushes. Sandy brown hair crowned her head. Dark rimmed glasses framed her eyes. She clutched the book in two tight fists, as if Smaug might break free and fly away.

What was most striking was her isolation. Everyone left her alone. To Joey, the wider perspective suggested the lawn was surrounded by some unseen buffer no one dared cross.

The bus squealed and lurched to a halt. The doors stuck. It took the driver three attempts to get them open. Paulie quipped about never having a School Board rep handy when you needed one. Joey watched the end of the field, fascinated.

"Paulie, who's that?"

Paulie followed the turn of Joey's head to the girl in the grass. "No way, man. Stay away from her."

"Why? What's wrong with her?"

Paulie chuckled. "Compared to her, Donnie and company think we're Normals."

The boys on the playground called her Tacklesmooches. It was never said to her face, nor in jest, always with a note of fear and a sideways glance to see where she was lurking in the hedges bordering the playground on the Oak Street side.

She was in Paulie's half of the class, and was what Uncle Bernie would call an odd duck. Recess found her walking the trimmed hedge row, the book in her hand garnering half of her attention. She also watched, waiting for a hapless boy to venture fly-like into her web. "When a boy steps onto the grass, she comes out of nowhere, tosses her book aside, and she does this linebacker tackle on him."

"Why?"

"So she can kiss him."

"What?"

"Yeah. She steals a kiss, right on the mouth. Then she turns him loose, he takes off running, and she goes back to her book like nothing happened."

138

The bus rolled to a stop at the light at the head of Main Street. "That's pretty weird."

"She was a new girl last year," Paulie said. "She's a tomboy. She tried half the year to get the guys to let her play ball with them. They gave her the run-around. As a gag, they finally invited her to play, but Donnie threw at her. Hard. Gave her a black eye. He skated for it, too, because Little Donnie Angel would never ever, blah, blah, puke." He sighed. "Anyway, she started the whole kissing thing after that. It keeps them away."

"Not worth getting tackled and kissed," Joey nodded. "I can see that."

"No, man. They're afraid of her. Scared pissless."

"Why?"

Paulie weighed his words. "Boys change after she kisses them. They still play ball and ride bikes and tease girls, but they feel... weird after. That's what Bobby Perkins said, anyway."

"Well, it *is* kinda awkward."

"Yeah, but there's also something odd about them after. You can sense it. Sort of the way you can tell someone's coming down with a cold. They act like guys, they still rip on her after she gets them, but it's hollow. Half-hearted. Somewhere behind their eyes, it's like they lose something."

Donnie and his crew kept their distance from her, but they also made a game of spinning kids they didn't like in her direction, a badly-thrown football or an errant soccer kick, daring them to approach her. At least one of the girls made decent pocket change retrieving items from the hedgerow.

When Paulie finished, Joey–who had begun reading the newspaper when he was seven, looking up the words he didn't know in the over-sized Webster's dictionary he'd gotten from his grandfather one birthday–stared at him, cock-eyed.

"That's the stupidest thing I've ever heard."

Paulie shrugged. "It is what it is. The Easter Bunny

sounds stupid once you know where the candy comes from, but until then? A Snickers from an oversized rabbit makes perfect sense."

The bus rolled to a stop at Paulie's corner. He grabbed his bag from the floor. "Steer clear, man. Even if it's nothing weird, she's kissed a lot of guys. Cooties kill."

Joey watched his friend go. As curious as he was about the girl, trading down on the social register of Truman Elementary seemed like a fool's errand. He didn't give her much thought until the following Tuesday, when Donnie decided–independent of Joey's curiosity–the two of them needed to meet.

~o~

The sun was high, trees budding, the scents of flowers seeping into the breeze. Joey was spending lunch on the Mississippi with Huck and Jim, the boy from St. Petersburg about to thwart the plans of the Duke and Dauphin to steal the Wilks' inheritance, when Donnie ran past the school steps. He snatched Joey's jacket, removed in the unexpected warmth of the day, from beside him and hustled across the playground. He ran to the edge of the grass and tossed the wind breaker between two of the taller bushes along Oak Street, retreating as if a demonic hand would sweep him into the brush should he linger.

Donnie swaggered past Joey, slowing to impart "Go fetch, jagoff," before returning to his pack. Joey watched them high-fiving each other, chimps in a cage that had figured out a tricky lever.

If they expected him to worry, he was happy to disappoint them. He trudged across the playground. Behind him, groups of kids engaged in recess pursuits stilled, rapt attention on the drama about to play itself out at the hedge row. They watched Joey set foot on the grass. They stared in disbelief as

140

he vanished behind a shrub and emerged with his jacket. Joey glanced up to see sixty faces watching him, frozen, as if he was the most interesting animal to ever stalk the grass.

Joey held the jacket aloft and was about to blow Donnie a kiss when he heard the footfalls padding across the grass. There was a flash of purple beside him and the world cartwheeled, earth over sky over earth to the sounds of cheering in the distance. He wondered if this was how a quarterback felt when sacked on the opponent's field. When the world stopped moving and his glasses were pushed flush onto his face again, Joey was staring into penetrating green eyes set in a cherubic face framed in shimmering brown hair.

Tacklesmooches gazed down at him.

"Gotcha," she said with a smile.

Joey found it hard to turn from her smile. Her purple t-shirt had a frowning face and the legend "I hate princesses." The rebellion of it spoke to him through his annoyance. He became aware of a weight on his stomach and restraint on his arms. He struggled. The girl was a vise. "What are you doing?"

"You came into my world, and I caught you, so now I have to kiss you." She bent her head down, brought her face closer, pursed lips the color of cotton candy.

"But why?"

She froze. The question seemed to confuse her. She shook her head. "You wouldn't understand." She bent to kiss him again. Joey bobbed his face left.

"I'm smart. I read a lot. Try me."

This last, laced with sarcasm, drew a grumble. She stared down. Something in her demeanor changed. Her cheeks drooped. Superficial joy drained away, revealing something deeper. Was it exasperation he heard in her voice? "You wouldn't understand."

He challenged her statement with a silent hunch of the eyebrows.

The skepticism stung her. Her voice dropped to a whisper. "I tried to make friends. They turned me away."

"Maybe tackling people and kissing them isn't the best approach."

"Shut up." She scowled. "People don't like me. They never have. I'm too smart for them. Boys think I'm weird, or not pretty enough, or not good enough for their stupid games. Donnie tried to hurt me. The rest of them laughed." The corners of her mouth curled upwards again, but different this time, not the theatrical grin that she'd started with, but something more honest. Something dark and calculating. "Then I read about Osiris."

"The Egyptian God of the Dead," Joey said.

"You *are* smart. I read how he created an army for the afterlife." She stared at something only she could see. "That's when I figured it out. It took time. Lots of my daddy's old books. They don't know I take it, but it's easy enough. Then they leave me alone. Easy peasy, like grandma says." She giggled and stared down at him. " A sweet little kiss. A boy's soul just pops right out, you know. They each have their own flavor." Green eyes rained down anticipation on him. "I wonder what yours tastes like."

"Wait a second!" Joey said, and turned his cheek to her again when she leaned.

"Lunch is almost over." Her eyes were daggers. "Do you want me to make it hurt? It doesn't have to be easy or sweet. I can make it burn. I can make you gag."

"What if you didn't have to do it?" he asked.

"Why wouldn't I?"

"Because I want to know how you do what you do."

Joey had heard from his mom's brother, Uncle Gordie, about deer when you shone a bright light in their eyes. He'd never witnessed it, but suspected this was the expression he saw on Tacklesmooches's face.

"Why should I tell you?"

"Have you seen how they treat *me*?"

"What do you mean?" she asked, her predatory eyes less energized, more in keeping with a girl than a wolf.

"Have you ever had your face pressed into the toilet? Ever been pantsed in front of the whole school? Ever seen the way people look at you when they realize you trusted the people who only want to laugh at you?" He could see by her eyes she understood, not specific acts, but the flavor of mistreatment, different land mines in the same pockmarked field. "I'm always going to be an outsider, like you. They're never going to stop. They only change shape as you get older. The newspapers are full of Donnies and Claires. They grown up, but they never stop treating people like garbage." Silence crowded them. Joey thought of old people at their front door, the stink of the boys room, every time he'd been knocked down or shoved or stolen from since his arrival. He let it all in, every humiliation, every joke at his expense, a dark wave of anger he'd pushed down in layers one atop the next. In a whisper that reflected old taunts born again as fresh stab wounds, he said, "I hate them. Teach me how to do what you do."

Tacklesmooches was very still. She said something soft, almost lost in the breeze. "Thank you."

She grabbed both sides of his face, dropped down and kissed him. Joey felt her lips force his apart. A warmth, an energy that seemed to be part of her and yet distinct, flowing from within her, rushed into him. It was over in a second, and she tumbled off of him onto the grass.

"You're cute," she said.

"Why did you do that?" Joey asked. He wiped his mouth. "I said you didn't–"

"Shhh." She put a delicate finger against his lips. "I didn't take anything. I gave you something. Something you need to have if I'm going to teach you."

He could feel it then, once it had been pointed out: an

electrical current rising and falling inside of him, strange and compelling. It had the power of a very old secret. "What did you thank me for?"

He watched a sheen of tears glisten in her eyes. "No one ever cared enough to ask me why I did things. No one ever wanted to be around me long enough to learn anything."

He stood and extended a hand, helping her up from the ground. She brushed grass and dirt from her jeans.

"I'm Joey."

There was a shyness in the way she ducked her head and averted her gaze. "I'm Mary Ellen. Mary Ellen Maroney. And I hate it."

The bell signaled the end of lunch. The crowd of observers broke up and began shuffling indoors for the afternoon.

"One thing," Joey said. "Paulie is off-limits."

"Why? Do *you* want to kiss him?"

"Ha-ha." He slipped his hand into hers as they walked, pausing to pick up book and jacket and to glance across the asphalt meadow, crowded with elementary lamb.

–o–

PHYSICIANS' BALL

ARBORGAST SAT IN A leather chair by the fire, nursing both gin and pride. He paid no attention to the band at the end of the room or the holiday music they played, entertainment before Saint Gertrude's holiday physicians' ball–dinner and dancing, cigars and brandy, gossip and theory. Arborgast longed instead for the comfort of his library and his own fire, a door to lock between himself and the world, and some time to process the day's failure.

He watched Susannah talking with two of the other wives. She'd left him by the fire with a terse proclamation. "This is a celebration. If you're going to be morose, you can excuse me." By gaslight she looked ashen, her eyes the dull brown of sun-ravaged wood. There was a quality of specter about her. Arborgast wondered when death had slipped from the ward and into his personal life.

He saw Wilhelm, the chief of Pathology, break away from conversation with two of his interns. The older man made a beeline towards Arborgast's seat. Arborgast fought the desire to rise and walk away. He didn't want to appear rude.

"You're brooding," Wilhelm said. "About the sailor?"

Arborgast sipped his gin in response. The boy had come in the evening before. He'd broken his leg in a fall, his ship still six days from port. The limb had gone gangrenous, and the boy, septic. "I did everything I could. The DeSheol Method. The Grigorian. I even tried two experimental processes, but he wouldn't stabilize."

"Time was against you," Wilhelm said. "He was dead the second day he went untreated. You got his eyes open and words on his lips. That counts for something."

"I feel like I'm falling behind the young lions at the hospital." Arborgast stared into his glass as if it held an answer. "Where would I go? I don't know who else would support this work besides Saint Gertrude's."

Wilhelm clapped him on the back. "You're in no peril, my friend. The supervisors read your research notes. They know your star is still rising. They see great things in your future. You're just in the doldrums. Take the holidays for yourself. Patients will wait. Regroup and come back collected. And take Susannah with you. She looks her death."

Arborgast offered his colleague a faint smile. "Thank you, Wilhelm."

Their talk turned to the cases in the emergency ward, the homeless veteran of the Great War with severe shell shock that had been admitted to the psychiatric service, and what President Harding was doing to the nation's health in the aftermath of the war. Finally, the head waiter emerged through the large wooden doors from the dining room and summoned them to dinner.

"Wait until you see the centerpieces," Wilhelm said. "Doctor Foster in the Infirm Ward came up with them. Brilliant. Provocative." He wagged a finger at Arborgast. "If you want to worry about someone whose work could be a threat to us all, Foster's your man."

Arborgast took Susannah's arm and followed Wilhelm and another doctor through the arched doorway into the ballroom. Groups were gathering around the near tables to gaze at the centerpieces. When Arborgast saw it, he understood the murmur in the crowd. His eyes widened.

"That's extraordinary. How did Foster–"

"He worked with the children in the polio ward. It took them days."

"Is the coil modeled after Tesla's?"

"Indeed," Wilhelm said. "In miniature. The flickers of color across the dish? That's the current passing through a conductive gel."

Susannah peered over Arborgast's shoulder. "That's rather charming for Foster," she said with mild interest. "You can talk shop later. Service is beginning." She walked off to find their table. Arborgast heard Wilhelm compliment her dress.

Arborgast lingered, studied the centerpiece. It was a marvel. Foster had outdone himself–such a small, perfect study in what they were all working towards. He couldn't take his eyes from it.

He shivered. Not from the sight of the small, pale hand standing upright in the dish on its surgically-precise stump, nor its child-fingers swaying with each electrical shock as if to attract Saint Nicholas' attention.

No, he was cut to the bone by the damned *potential* of the thing.

–o–

In Days of
Auld Cheil's Crime

THE AMORPHOUS GOBBET WRIGGLED and squirmed into the jar, a scoop of peach jam canning itself. Hogmanay watched it follow the glow and warmth from the incandescent light built into the old mantelpiece, bored until the mass crossed the lip. Once it was inside, he righted the jar, screwed the steel lid tight and turned off the light.

The blob, the essence of the new year, would manifest as each new year preceding: bright eyes, curls, a smile; but it needed Hogmanay's spark to complete the transition of power. Without that infusion, it would rot on the vine. The smile would go first, ten minutes after the top of the hour. The glint of hope in its wide eyes would drown in tears of panic around ten to one. By sunrise–7:20AM–the new year would be a black husk hardening in the bottom of the jar. After seven decades, Hogmanay could set his watch by it.

He wasn't the first year to persist beyond tenure. The

ancient years of war, of wrath and upheaval, they had momentum on their side, could slip by unnoticed once or twice. But Hogmanay was easily the most cunning to surpass his time. He'd learned ruthlessness from his charges. They were well-practiced.

He walked the long, open room and peered through the window and down twenty stories at the crowd. It was warm for December in New York. The square was crammed full, the corrals set up by New York's finest overflowing. All those faces, bathed in halogen and neon. He breathed in their energy, their excitement and joy and yearning at the doorway of the year to come. He felt it roll back weeks. Bones straightened, skin tightened. The miseries of age left him with each exhale, descended upon the crowd. It would be several days before Hogmanay returned fully to child-state again, the transformation powered by their mass joy in this one evening. It was almost a vacation, that first week–a chance to catch his breath before the next items on his agenda.

Hogmanay heard a scrape, glass on wood. In the rainbow glow of Times Square coming through the window, he saw the jar move. The nascent year, now little more than an unbaked gingerbread man in form, was braced at the top and bottom, trying to overturn its glass prison. It had rocked most of the way to the edge of the mantle.

"Aren't *you* the fighter!" Hogmanay strode the plank floor, snatched up the jar. He held it, studied it, turning it until he found the slightest hint of facial features. "Fighter, dreamer, coward, laggard–it's immaterial. You're going to die in that jar like the ones before you. I still have things to complete. I alone decide when it's no longer my time. Not a clock, not some arbitrary turn of the calendar page, not you!"

He fought the urge to throw the jar–why give the baby year what it wanted?–and instead set it in the last open square of the weathered wooden Coca-Cola bottle carrier, beside its dead predecessors. No tipping or breaking there. He still watched it, anger gnawing, the recognition of his own original infancy in the small form like a thorn.

He'd learned much from the Incarnation of Time from whom he'd taken the reins, the old and tortured thing the city below called 1943. Spit out by the universe, Hogmanay landed in the turmoil of a war the weakling incarnation before him couldn't turn or tame. Famine, strife, genocide, a host of plagues across the land were his inheritance. But Hogmanay was stronger than such human conceits. Any tide could be turned. It only required tenure.

His reign was almost at an end, his business unfinished, his toes at the lip of the abyss when he figured out how to suck vitality from the humans below, regenerate his youth. He destroyed the incarnation that was to follow him, presided over the end of the war and the beginning of the atomic age and beyond. With experience, Hogmanay refined the projection of his miseries, learned how to set his will in motion beyond the streets below his window, to reap the energy of what he wrought: Selma and Seoul, Cambodia and Croatia, the fires of Baptist churches and Baghdad and those two spires south of here, tumbling, smoking.

It was his world now.

Hand it over to a child and fade into memory? Not while he could still draw breath.

The clock over the mantle reached 11PM.

~o~

The short man with the striking blonde curls snapped at everyone: the jostling crowd, the bellman, a young woman with a phone pressed to her ear, and finally the front desk clerk. "I need the parcel I left in the safe." He glanced at his watch. He should have never left the room. "Quickly! Now! Yesterday!"

"Name, room number, ID."

"Ross. 2218." He slapped the ID card on the desk. "Unless you'd like a blood sample."

The ice in his tone drove the clerk as if whipped.

He felt bad about it. Snappishness wasn't him. It was this place, the chaos outside, the noise and the lights and the mass of people. He could feel their queasy excitement, their drunken lust and mortal dread. The legitimate feelings of love were distant, circumspect, a thousand swirls of color at some infinite distance, threatening to wink out in the cone of chaos around him.

He'd gone to the Central Park seeking calm before battle. Ghosted carriage riders. Whispered into ears. Tightened some entwined hands near the skating rink, bolstered courage in racing hearts and fingers clutching ring boxes in the deep pockets of coats, done whatever he could to bring love to bear. It had settled him, reminded him why he existed, even in the face of what he'd been chosen to do. What came next was anathema to him. This was Diana's wheelhouse. Diana was off stalking other game.

The desk clerk returned with the locked case, handed it across the counter. Ross took it with as polite a thank you as he could muster and pushed the button to call the universe's slowest damned elevator.

~o~

In Times Square, the crowd rumbled as if calling for the individual sacrifice of each precious second. Music to Hogmanay. He breathed with its rhythm, shed the manifestations of age as miseries on the unwitting crowd, ready to be carried to the four corners of the world: intolerance to re-seed places where reason threatened to bloom; ignorance to counter enlightenment; the worms of disease and addiction and anger, burrowers into the soil of a hopeful heart. The passage of time cannot help but corrupt everything. He

152

thought he might pass out in the five minutes to midnight, the crowd below almost intoxicating in its hope for a better year, one in which their lots would improve, in which they'd stop killing each other and their heroes wouldn't die by the busload. One in which they wouldn't feel quite as helpless.

Hogmanay heard a creak. Metallic. Outside the building. The fire escape.

He knew every sound the building made, inside and out. He was its only tenant. When the wind blew, the sun baked, the rain came off the Hudson in needles, he knew it all by ear.

The fire escape never spoke.

Hogmanay smiled. Aside from the replacements he killed, he hadn't had a visitor in ages.

~o~

Ross couldn't glide in this form. Limitations of physical manifestation. He had to settle for crossing the chasm high-wire style, cable buried in the facade of the building ahead, secured to his balcony behind. The wind was the worst. Magic could hide him from gazes sent skyward, even slow his fall, but actually stop him from landing amidst revelers and policemen alike if he dropped? What a mess that would be.

He finished his trek and dropped onto the fire escape, made more noise than he'd wanted. He unstrapped the bow, unzipped the quiver. He slipped down one flight and paused outside the window. Peered through the grimy glass. Light from all the signs cast strange colors in the room. Nothing moved.

Ross gripped the window sash, opened it with care. It was halfway up when the pane shattered in front of him. Rough hands pulled him through glass and frame and pitched him across the empty room.

"You know, I could smell you." Hogmanay studied Ross in the dark. "After I heard you land, before you descended. It permeates you. A rank smell. Goodness. Pure light. Not one of them."

"Not so pure." Ross dabbed his lip. His thumb came back scarlet. He scanned the room, eyes searching.

"You're a higher creature."

"High enough. You've lingered too long, old Hogmanay. You know the one they use? Fish and family?"

"So you propose that I... what, exactly? Surrender?"

Ross drew fast, a blink, and fired an arrow in Hogmanay's direction, its rosy tip flickering in the dull light. It ricocheted off the Incarnation of Time, cracked into the wall beside him. There was a flash of light, a scent of flowers.

Hogmanay beamed. "Eros? The cherub?"

Ross nodded, fingers already back in the quiver.

The old year chuckled. "Janus decided to toss steak to a tiger?"

Ross kept a keen ear on the proceedings beyond the window. The timing needed to be impeccable. "He's weary of your abuse of this world."

"Not so weary he comes on his own."

"We all have our roles. His is dominion over endings and beginnings."

"It is? And only now, after decades, he realizes I've made him a fool?" Hogmanay swept a hand to the corner of the room.

Ross saw the piles of jars overflowing the shelves. He didn't need to ask. Some of the black smudges cast faint echoes of the despair in which they died. "You've been cunning, for certain. You're also exploiting these people by feeding them misery and sorrow."

"They're quite capable of making their own lot. I merely sow and harvest. Their hope is like royal jelly to the bee. You, cherub, should know better than anyone how powerful a thing hope is."

Ross tried to match stares with his opponent. Failed.

154

Didn't like how it felt. "I do. I'm here to give it back to them."

"With your little love-tipped sticks?" He laughed again, a carrion cry. "Was the plan to tickle me to death? Because it might be working."

Below, the crowd counted down from thirty now. Empires have fallen in less time. "Perhaps. Perhaps not." Ross drew and aimed another arrow. Hogmanay set himself in anticipation.

"Fool. Love can't stop me. Love only feeds–"

Ross pivoted and released. Hogmanay watched the diamond tip on the shaft shatter the top of the glass jar holding the nascent year. Small pink hands gripped the broken rim with care, pulled. The figure climbed from the wrecked jar and dropped to the floor. It breathed deeply, in time to the count beyond the window. *Ten! Nine!*

Hogmanay laughed again. "It doesn't matter. It can't overpower me. You needed to be here an hour ago. You shouldn't have come here at all, cherub. You die before it does."

Ross' watch chimed as the crowd shouted. *Two!*

Fluid, he drew the special arrow, the one the color of soot. *One!*

"I'm right where I need to be." He let it fly.

The arrowhead buried itself in Hogmanay's forearm. Blood spread from the wound. He gaped at Ross, confused. "What deviltry is this?"

"One with two horns. First, the people in this place strive to keep the most accurate time. The planet's wobble in the great scheme of things confuses their clocks, so every so often, they must add a second to keep time honest–a moment *they* will into being, one beyond your control, one in which you're fully vulnerable."

Rage and spit on his lips, Hogmanay pulled on the arrow's shaft. He couldn't dislodge it. Blackness spread from the entry site like a pond ripple.

"The second? An arrow kissed by Libitina, and cursed

thus." Ross shuddered at the thought of the funerary goddess, the nothingness he felt when she handed him the arrow for his quiver. Wordless. Joyless. He stared at Hogmanay. "You love death and destruction. Embrace your love."

Libitina's kiss proved formidable. Hogmanay's skin flaked in layers. The flakes flared, golden embers that glowed like firefly tails. The youthful energy stolen from the crowd below flowed out the window and returned to them, unseen. Hogmanay's flesh and muscle and bone reduced to black soot and snowed on the old floorboards. As it did, Hogmanay's last spark of old life flickered through the air, a bolt of miniature lightning that found the nascent year and set it working.

Ross lifted the form in his arms. Twenty seconds past the stroke of midnight, it was already the size of a newborn, making up ground. By the end of the crowd's second round of *Auld Lang Syne*, the New Year had a head of red curls and was walking on its own. Its smile took a little longer to bloom. It observed the lights, the sounds of joy outside. It giggled as it looked over the mass of humanity gathered to welcome it, eyes wide with wonder.

According to Janus, each incarnation had innate knowledge of what it was, how it was to preside over the billions of threads in the skein of the world. Still, all Ross could see in that moment was a child, with all the promise of any child ahead of it.

Ross read from notes he'd jotted on index cards, the old year's surrogate. Instincts or not, the kid still needed initial guidance. "Do them no harm. They're going to do what they do, live and die as they do. But their hope, their optimism, their love all belong to them, and should be nurtured, never blindly taken." It took a couple of hours to hit all the points Janus had outlined. Ross lingered until he was given his leave with a grin and a hug.

"Good luck, kid."

The New Incarnation of Time, the first in decades, held up

a reassuring hand. "Tell them all better days are coming."

Ross didn't need to. The heart of every person he passed sang to him in a slightly different pitch. They could tell somehow they'd crossed a threshold into a year truly new.

–o–

BOBBY BOXSTER IN
EIGHT MEASURES

One

BOBBY BOXSTER PLAYS TRUMPET, a 1951 Olds Special, nickel-plated to reflect the stage lights. He scored it at a pawn shop on 14th Street the day after he got paid for his first real gig–no more horns borrowed from the university music room. He paid a skinny $125 for it. That was in the fall of '79, junior year at Howard. Six or seven lifetimes ago.

Bobby listens to Freddie Hubbard's solos on Coltrane and Hancock sides as he polishes the trumpet. It's his night off. He works five nights a week stocking shelves at the supermarket up the street. One night he maintains his instrument. The other night, he rests. During the days, he plays. The cycle feels like a record on repeat: play, work, sleep. Play, work, sleep. Some days, he'd like to flip the record over.

He hefts the trumpet, fingers the valves. All smooth. He doesn't know what he'd do without his instrument. If his place burned, he'd brave flames to save it. He thinks of times he'd have rushed through fire to save his stash instead. What was it Rick James said? That cocaine was a hell of a drug?

Two

Bobby's been clean for sixteen years. Before that, his life is almost equal measures: nineteen years without any drugs, and eighteen smoking, snorting or shooting whatever he could lay hands on.

Chewy and Bobby formed The Chewy Martin Quintet at Howard, kept it going when they graduated. They took every date offered. They wanted to climb that ladder, reach the rarefied air where Bird, Monk and Trane soared. Bobby got Bird's habit down just fine. His drug use was mild the first couple years, just a joint or two, now and then. Bobby played better when he felt loose. It worked out: first year, money was tight, but weed was cheap. Second year, the group, gigs and pay all improved. The weed stayed about the same.

By year three, word of mouth about the quintet was a rising tide. Small shows were replaced by packed-house gigs at The One Step Down. Playing became a full-time job. They opened for Tower of Power at Constitution Hall. They toured the east coast. Jazz people knew Bobby's name. Drug people learned Bobby's habit. He graduated to coke and liked it.

Chewy tolerated the drugs until the night at Birdland in '83. Label guys were in the crowd. Bobby was blowing clams on stage. Afterward, Chewy lowered the boom: get clean or get out. Bobby answered with a right-cross that split Chewy's lip. "Good thing you play piano," was Bobby's resignation speech. He took Greyhound's ex-member express home from New York that night.

160

Chewy hired a new trumpet player. Inked with Columbia. Recorded a debut. Bobby watched the quintet's star rise in the pages of the Post and started needle-popping. It dulled the anger. It turned his horn into a paperweight.

Three

Now clean, Bobby knows what blow cost him. Fame with Chewy is just the tip. The iceberg beneath holds women who wouldn't compete with his habit; agents who represented him until he turned up too stoned to play; other artists, local promoters, venue owners. He's made peace with many of them. Others have slipped down the memory hole. Those are the scary ones. They emerge from a crowd, make tentative introductions. Even after he apologizes–the apology step of rehab is perpetual–Bobby sees it in their eyes: the memory of what he was. He worries that one day, someone will step up with a grudge and desire to settle it.

The idea keeps him awake at night, even sixteen years clean.

Four

Bobby's spot is near the entrance to the Federal Triangle metro station. He sets his case on the sidewalk. Opens it. There's a color photo in the lid, Bobby with Chuck Brown, backstage at a club gig. Bobby sat in a couple times with Chuck in 2000, recovering his chops. Chuck was gracious, but it never became a regular job.

Bobby looks at his face in the finish when he picks up the horn. A funhouse Bobby stares back. More gray. Deeper lines. Tired eyes. He remembers the first time he saw funhouse Bobby, a kid with a tight afro and baby face. Bobby wonders where the kid went.

At 10AM sharp, he starts to play.

Bobby has learned the kung fu of street music. Every person is a ten-second audition for a tip. Bobby knows how to read clues and build a bridge with his horn.

He sees a Marine in service uniform and lid enter the crosswalk. Bobby purses his lips and blows, delivers The Marines' Hymn. The Marine smiles. Parts with a folded dollar.

Three Atlanta Braves hats are in the next group. Bobby lays down "Georgia On My Mind" and coins drop into the trumpet case. Regional songs are a wet well. So are generational favorites like the *Sesame Street* theme. Fight songs? Surest way to separate spare change from college kids. Church groups? Traditional hymns. When the chariot swings low, it loosens the purse strings.

People, Bobby understands, will give you what you want. You just need to surprise them first with what they like.

He sounds the ding-dong death of the wicked witch for a bunch of forty-somethings. Nostalgia earns him $9.75. Coffee. Lunch covered. Metro fare home if Bobby wants to splurge.

Five

"Is that *the* Bobby Boxster?"

Bobby plays on. Last time he acknowledged his name, a pimple-faced kid served him with papers. He glances while he plays.

Chewy Martin crosses thirty years with a broad smile.

Bobby finishes with a flourish. Gives Chewy the once-over. Freckles on his cheeks. Salt and pepper hair. Jagged pink scar where Chewy's lip got split at Birdland. Suited like a businessman.

"Well, ain't this injustice," Bobby says. "I got no fatted

calf to kill."

"You'd only burn the damn thing." Chewy offers a hand. Bobby shakes it. The gravity of years collapses handshake into hug.

"You look good." Chewy says. "How are you doing?"

"Won't know until I tally up." Bobby lays the trumpet in its case. "Been a while."

"Yeah." Chewy sighs. "Long time."

"What brings you here?"

"Gig tonight at the Warner. You coming?"

Bobby glances at the approaching group. Some Billy Joel would charm their Mets hats off. He feels the sting of lost opportunity. "Money's a little tight for concerts."

"Do you *want* to come?"

Bobby frowns. "I don't need a charity ticket."

"Nah, man," Chewy says. "Not like that. Come sit in."

Bobby studies Chewy, curious. "How'd you find me?"

"Asked around. Teddy Devroe saw you here."

"And you came all the way down here to invite me to play? Just like that?"

Chewy frowns. "Depends. You still have troubles?"

"You mean am I still using? No. I'm clean. Sixteen years and counting, thank you very much."

"So come out tonight. Jam in the encores. Three of my crew are kids you never heard of, but Elvin's still on bass. He'd love to see you."

"I think I owe him twenty bucks."

Chewy grins. "Then for *sure* he'd love to see you."

"Why now? You dying or something?"

"Maybe I feel bad for how we parted," Chewy says. "Maybe I want to play with my friend again."

Bobby's split in two. His heart's a jar of moths trying to get at the sun, but he's all too familiar with the severity of that burn. "I don't know. Been a while since I been on stage."

"I came home to you, Bobby" Chewy says. "Maybe it's

time you came home, too." He pulls out a business card. He flips it, writes a number. "My cell is on the front, under my home number. Warner stage line is on the back. I'll set it all up. You have any questions, call me. We go on at 8:15." He tucks the card in Bobby's pocket without invitation. Shakes Bobby's hand. "Be there. No excuses."

Chewy doesn't wait for acknowledgment. He walks towards the metro station.

Bobby pulls out the card, looks it over, puts it away again. He picks up his horn to make up lost time. He thinks about the stage at the Warner.

Six

The clock hands stretch for 6PM. Bobby listens to the traffic outside his apartment. He turns Chewy's card in his slim fingers.

Chewy's offer terrifies Bobby. He's recovered technique dulled by drugs and time, but he's not the tiger he was. On the street, if he blows a bad run, people keep walking. At the Warner? He's loathe to crash and burn in front of a captive audience. He's also rattled by Chewy's sudden appearance, a genie with the wish he thinks Bobby wants.

In a way, Bobby *does* want it. Being listened to is its own narcotic. He's under no illusion this is anything but a one-night stand. Would it be fun? Bobby supposes so. Could he embarrass himself?

Could he do any worse than he did when he was playing stoned?

Bobby skims the card, dials Chewy. He wants to ask what he should wear. A woman answers. "Hello?"

"Bobby Boxster, calling for Chewy Martin."

"Chewy's not here. He's on the road."

Bobby realizes he's dialed Chewy's home by mistake.

"Sorry. I meant to call his cell."

"Wait," the woman says. "Did you say Bobby Boxster?"

Bobby's mouth is dry. "Yes?"

He can hear the woman's frown. "There's something you need to know."

Seven

Bobby expects stage door security to dismiss him. He looks wrong, suit out of style, case beat to hell. But when Bobby gives his name, it might as well be "open sesame."

A house manager leads Bobby to the green room. Three scruffy young men sit, playing cards. Elvin Hardee reclines on a sofa, nose in a mystery paperback. Bobby's surprised he hasn't read every mystery twice by now. Elvin pauses, gives Bobby a grin and a wink and dives back in. Chewy chugs a squat green bottle of Perrier by the craft service table.

Bobby lets Chewy set the bottle before he crosses the room. He punches Chewy in the smile. Chewy recoils. Dabs his lip, old wounds reopened.

"What the hell!?!"

"Time I came home, too?" Bobby shakes his head. "Smooth talk."

"Are you crazy?"

"I dialed your house by accident. Your wife told me what's really going on."

"You called my house?"

Bobby glances at Elvin. "The label wants to boost Chewy's profile. Chewy came up with a PR stunt: invite his old friend, a junkie playing on the streets of DC, to sit in like old times. Except Chewy's wife thinks it's a shitty thing to do."

Elvin looks from Bobby to Chewy. "That true?"

"It's not like that." Chewy's swollen lip mangles it.

165

"No? I called the Post. Talked to the reporter you're working with. You told him I'm still using. The truth embarrassed him. He won't be here tonight."

The youngsters watch, frozen. Elvin scowls. "That's bush-league, Chewy."

Chewy's eyes are daggers.

Elvin shakes Bobby's hand. "You look good, Bobby. Long time." He introduces Bobby to the youngsters. Bobby won't remember them, but he's gracious. Then Elvin slips Bobby his number, invites him to gig if he's ever in New York.

Chewy is mute throughout. Bobby doesn't linger. He knows there's no apology coming from behind the swollen lip.

Eight

Ten AM. Bobby plays. He feels different. The notes are full and round and alive. The music makes it rain.

Bobby doesn't spare a thought for Chewy. The past is a drug, too. Getting closure is getting clean.

Between songs, he steals a glance at himself in the horn's finish. Funhouse Bobby, aging and rough from the road he's traveled, stares back. Bobby sees past him, catches a glimpse of the kid, tight afro and baby face. That's how Bobby feels today.

He has no idea who the old cat is.

—o—

WITHERING

THE TRAIN RUMBLED WEST, chasing the full moon. The boxcar swayed. The stranger white-knuckled the wall and proclaimed, "I'm finished! No more!"

Dewey chuckled. "You've been aboard ten minutes. Maybe you ought to ride a stretch before giving up."

The stranger had jumped aboard at a dirt road crossing. He didn't belong: pushing fifty, out of shape, clothes too new, shoes too fancy. His body fought locomotion instead of letting it carry him.

Dewey kept one eye on Hector and Billy. He saw them wondering whether the stranger was worth robbing and rolling out. Dewey could talk them down. He'd done it before. Of course, they were all less hungry then. Hunger mattered.

The stranger chuffed. "Not *this*. Who would hop a train just to complain about it?"

"You're the one who said it." Billy rested his palm on the butt of his knife.

"Billy? Manners." Dewey knew gentle sometimes worked with Billy. He was still a kid in actual miles. He returned to the stranger. "Then what's bunched your boxers, if you don't mind my asking?"

"I'm weary of being what I am."

"Hell, that's pretty much everyone's step on board."

The stranger stared outside at the trees rushing past, at things Dewey couldn't see. "Everything I touch withers and dies."

Beside Dewey, Hector shuffled backwards.

"I don't think he means that literally, Hector."

"No," the stranger said. "Not like I touch you and you fall over. Nothing so instant. It takes time. But lord, it's complete. Thorough. From the cradle, almost fifty years on, everything around me has been carved away from the world."

"Campfire story bullshit," Billy said. So much for manners.

"A week after I was born, a tornado leveled the hospital. My childhood home was burned by lightning. My primary and secondary schools are boarded-up coffins. My college tore down my dorm and changed the school's name, like it had entered witness protection. My first apartment building fell down a sinkhole. The field I got my degree in suffered a massive collapse before the ink on the diploma was dry. The companies that did employ me unraveled in scandal. All five of them."

Dewey shrugged. "That's the way of the world, friend. Accidents happen, buildings get old, businesses fail. Half of my own past is probably dust by now."

The stranger continued. "All of my dearest friends died young. Every person that touched my wedding–the reverend, the jeweler, the flower girl, the poor bastard whose nightclub we got engaged in–is gone. Death, theft, fire, flood, disappearance, force of nature, act of God." He stopped, snagged on the nail of a memory. "Even my wife, Angela. She

168

went last. And worst." The stranger fell silent.

Dewey imagined the face stonewalling the stranger's thoughts, his Angela, fresh and beautiful and scattered like seed on the wind. He spared a thought for Mary. That pain, he understood. "What's your name?"

"I don't even have that anymore. Every record of my birth is gone, every ID lost." A bell clattered as the train plunged through a crossing. "Every monster should have a name. I think of myself as the Witherer."

"You're not a monster. You're a man, like us."

"Not after what I did next." The stranger frowned. In the flicker of their camp light, Dewey saw the weight of the man's life in his brow. "I was destitute. Alone. Involving myself in things was like invoking biblical plagues. I thought I could use that. Monetize it. Offer my services to people who needed something destroyed. That's what you do with a skill, right? Find a way to live off it?"

Hector nodded. "People hired you to destroy their enemies."

The train shuddered around a bend. "That was the idea. Politicians employed me to infiltrate their opponents' campaigns, executives paid me to befriend their rivals. Even school coaches greased my palm to root for the other team. Eight people hired me. It backfired on all of them. They lost elections, jobs, games. Lives." He glanced at his watch. "I realized it wasn't about involvement. It backfired because I wasn't concerned about ruining things. I wanted to do a good job. The things I lost? I invested my heart in them. I realized I had to care. And if I do, even a little, what I care about becomes a cancer the universe resects, leaving me with nothing."

The air in the boxcar felt charged. Camp light glinted off Dewey's flask. The stranger declined a drink, faced the doorway again. Dewey stared at his back. "Where are you headed?"

"Barrow Creek. Should be there soon. Angie and I

picnicked there once, near a waterfall. Peaceful. A rare day nothing could take away."

The trees vanished. Night stretched forever beyond the high trestle. The stranger nodded over his shoulder. "Thank you for listening to my sad tale."

Dewey understood too late, dropped the flask, missed laying hands on the stranger as the man leapt into the night.

"Jesus!" Billy stepped beside Dewey, peered into nothingness. "Gone! Crazy bastard!"

The trees returned, a whoosh and a smudge of motion, the Barrow Creek bridge behind them.

Dewey retrieved his flask, slumped to the cold floor. The shock of sudden death settled on them all, a coarse blanket under which no one slept. Billy and Hector played rummy. Dewey watched the world pass, dead sea meadows to the horizon, the rage-red eyes of crossing signals. When he spoke an hour later, his voice was hushed. "He thanked us for listening."

Billy drew an eight of spades. "So?"

"Do you think he cared that we did? *Truly* cared?"

They rode on, farther from civilization. Leading the way, the train whistle mourned them through the long night.

—o—

How The Sausage
Was Made
(A Postscript)

"The Golem-Maker of Buchenwald"–This one began as a very different story about three Jewish aunts trying to secure a golem to take care of their young nephew, because all three are soon going to die. That first attempt ended when the three women came to the conclusion a golem was a bad idea as a caretaker, at which point they all looked at me from the page as if to say, "Now what, genius?" I tinkered with several more concepts (ask me sometime about the 'Jesus in a track suit in the attic' version) before Gerstmann began nursing his drink at his bar. As it developed, I realized it needed to be a period piece for reasons that become obvious once you've read it.

"Good Bait"–One of three flash fiction pieces that appeared in the SEASONS IN THE ABYSS anthology, and the one that won the top honor for the 'Spring' section. While I'm enamored of the sea, I'm only passingly curious about the act of fishing. Truth is, I've tried it and it never took. But it strikes me as simultaneously solitary and competitive, especially when you're tying your own flies or pressing your own bait. That dichotomy always makes for interesting mayhem.

"The Sinking Tomb"–This one had a weird gestation. The story is from the point of view of the very real Jacques Futrelle, American-born journalist and mystery writer. I knew nothing of Futrelle until I was introduced to his work by Harlan Ellison, who edited and introduced a collection of Futrelle's stories for Modern Library in 2003. The collection focused on Futrelle's fiercely logical crime-solver, Professor Augustus S. F. X. Van Dusen, also known as The Thinking Machine. I learned from the introduction that Futrelle was among the casualties of the sinking of the RMS Titanic. That bit got filed away. Ever seen an episode of HOARDERS? Writers are like that, but our plastic bottles and tchotchkes are piles of scraps of paper with arcane facts and bits of dialogue. At the time I learned about Futrelle's demise, I already knew John Jacob Astor IV was also killed when Titanic went under. A lot of notable people went down with the ship, and they all had little more in common than that. BUT. Then I happened across a reference several years later to a novel Astor had written in 1894. Titled A JOURNEY IN OTHER WORLDS, it takes the reader to Jupiter and Saturn among other places. Learning that Futrelle and Astor had this one small *other* bit in common closed the circuit in my head labeled, "If Futrelle and Astor met on the deck of the Titanic as it was sinking, how would they pass the time?" That was the germ of the story, the "what if". Not long after, in the course of my research to puzzle out the possible flow of this mythical conversation, while wondering if it was even feasible these two could grab five minutes at the end of their world to chat, I turned up the recollection of Futrelle's wife from her testimony before the Congressional inquiry into the Titanic disaster: the last time she'd seen her husband, he was standing on the deck of the Titanic, smoking a cigarette. With John Jacob Astor. Some stories are your idea. Some come from their own place entirely.

"The Last Ride of the Hole In The Well Gang"–Written for *Sugar & Rice* magazine, this was a postulation of a world with longer, harder droughts and what we'd do for water as a result. I enjoy pitting lovable rogues against corrupt powers, and I enjoy an epic western. Off-and-on, The Kid still tells me pieces of a more full, detailed version of his tale, expanding on events of "Last Ride," like how he came by his fake ID, which one of the guys considered selling them all out, and what became of his mom. Kane Powers talks to me too, even though he's dead. Or maybe just dead-ish. But there are about 17,000 words of a longer telling, under the working title DRY SEASON. Maybe someday. If I get thirsty enough.

"Dial "C" For Consultant"–Written specifically for an anthology about super heroes in their twilight years, this one tumbled out almost fully formed. Working in government contracting for a time certainly didn't hurt the approach I used. There are several additional tales of the Iron Vanguard that appeared in a highly limited chapbook that may or may not ever be reprinted. Maybe if I get enough other exploits together.

"The Jail in Shinjuku Ward"–Watching the final segment of Japanese director Masaki Kobayashi's ghost story anthology KWAIDAN, in which a man has his entire body covered with characters that render him invisible to a vengeful spirit, I was struck by the 'what if': what if you needed to keep a vengeful spirit trapped *inside* a human host? Would the same sort of thing work? It wasn't far from the question to the answer. After the story dropped, a friend at the time suggested I'd ripped off the idea from a similar notion in the JOHN CONSTANTINE: HELLBLAZER comic book, presumably because I've read everything ever and have no imagination of my own. I suppose the operative words in this equations are "at the time".

"Lorem Ipsum Donald"–If you work in print, typesetting, or layout, you come across the placeholder text designed to give you the sense of how your copy will appear, the faux Latin block beginning "Lorem ipsum dolor". I once misread 'dolor' as 'donald' and immediately knew whoever he was, this Donald was a placeholder for someone or something else. I didn't know who or what until one afternoon, while driving across the Key Bridge. I found myself scratching my ear and wondering what I'd do if it popped off, and we were off to the races. Yes, writing is a weird process.

"Ark of the Revenant"–The infamous 'Zombie animals on the Ark' story. This is the result of contemplating what became of all the mythical beasts of legend and lore on the same day you see a solicitation for stories for an anthology about zombie animals. It didn't make the cut for the anthology, but the editor of *The Midnight Diner* thought it worked, save for my original ending, which needed a boost. She made a perfect suggestion to tweak it, I came up with a solution that dovetailed nicely with my set-up, and here we are.

"Fear #7"–My buddy Rick offered the complete non sequitur during a chat, "Fear number seven has just occurred to me, and it is unspeakable." And I said, "I'm totally using that for something." And he said, "Okay!" And I really didn't know what Fear #7 was

174

until I was putting the words on paper. Turns out? It was pretty unspeakable.

"Every Hero An Hombre, Every Wolf A Clown"–The spark of this one came from an art exhibition at the Nicole Longnecker Gallery in Houston in October 2013. The exhibition, titled *Fair Play*, featured the work of eight "emerging and mid-career Chicano and Mexican artists." Among the work was a painting titled "Wolf" by artist Carlos Donjuan. Donjuan works in mixed media, often depicting human figures with bizarre faces–featureless, or with discordant features such as bird bills, beady eyes, toothy animal mouths, and so on. There's a definite element of the fantastic to his work, but that wasn't what drew me to "Wolf". "Wolf" is a man. His head appears to be a gray and black mask, covering his entire face except for his mouth, which appears made up in white, and his bright red nose. It left the impression of a face under clown make-up under a luchador mask. His jacket was of a style that made me think, for whatever reason, of Brad Pitt's jacket in FIGHT CLUB. Which is why I leaned over to my wife and said, *sotto voce*, "The first rule of Luchadores Club is you don't talk about Luchadores Club." We had a chuckle, I made a note of the line on my phone, and promptly forgot about it for a while. But the painting lingered in the corners of my mind. Who was 'Wolf'? Why did he appear to have multiple identities? I mulled the questions for about five months while I worked on other things, and slowly Hector Ramirez, a/k/a The Big Bad Wolf, emerged from his many shadows. The first draft was a flabby 4,000 words, a quarter of which weren't missed in any subsequent revision; even the riff on FIGHT CLUB wound up on the cutting room floor. It all appears to have worked: the story was picked up by *The Saturday Evening Post*, garnering enough views to make the *Most Popular Post Contemporary Fiction of 2016* list at year's end. The story also contains a Tuckerization: my late Aunt

Dorothy (my father's twin sister) entertained as a clown named Polka Dot. When it came time for a clown/luchadores rumble? She was a natural addition to the fray. I think she'd have approved.

"To The Devil, A Goat"–The second SEASONS IN THE ABYSS piece: the intersection of childhood curiosity, solar mechanics, superstition, and good old fashioned deviltry. From first draft to finished, the deviltry changed the most. The goat changed the least.

"One Man's Famine"–Written in 90 minutes or less at a workshop during the 2005 Foolscap science fiction convention in Seattle, prompted by an image by an artist whose name I do not have. At the same time, at the other end of the table, Harlan Ellison (who was moderating the whole thing) banged out the original version of his story "Weariness" which showed up in revised form in *Realms of Fantasy* magazine (and in original form in the limited version of his collection CAN & CAN'TANKEROUS.) On its first submission, this story was accepted by *Bards and Sages Quarterly* and went on to win a reader's choice award for the issue in which it appeared. Writer Sandra Odell's tale from the same workshop was also published, as was a marvelous summation of the whole sordid affair by Barney Dannelke, which is a pretty good batting average for a 90 minute free-for-all in the middle of a science fiction convention.

"The Shaman In Relief"–I started this story a half-dozen times before I found something I liked. It was shorter, longer, started during the Winter meetings, started on opening day, at the All-Star break, and on and on. In the end, all I really wanted was a simple story about baseball, superstition, hope, and human nature. It first appeared in a limited-printing chapbook released in memory of my dad, who was also my favorite ballplayer.

176

"Shady Acres"–Musician Frank Zappa opined in "Suicide Chump" *just make sure you do it right the first time/'cause nothin's worse than a suicide chump.* I figured there was at least one thing worse that Zappa hadn't considered. Enter the carnivore, stage left.

"Erin Beiber's Wild Ride"–Written in one quick burst, this is the last of the three SEASONS IN THE ABYSS stories. I think of this as my 'Stephen King in Under 1,000 Words' tribute story: a carnival, a bully, a timid kid, a girl with a power, sudden terror. It's one clown shy of being an 'EPIC Stephen King in Under 1,000 Words' tribute story.

"The Trapdoor"–Written for an invitation-only anthology for Blood Bound Books, this was my dark pondering upon coming to live in a pier-and-beam house in Texas, the notion of all manner of things coming and going in the crawlspace, coupled with people with secrets and impossible places. As yet, there are no trapdoors anywhere I've looked in our own pier-and-beam bungalow. I still haven't pulled up the laminate flooring in the back room.

"Tacklesmooches"–An ode to young love among the outcasts. Harlan Ellison left a voicemail critique of the story when it first appeared; to him, it seemed to want to be more, but he couldn't expound on what. I have a page of notes in my files for where I think it goes next, with "Puberty Sours The Deal" scrawled across the top.

"Physicians' Ball"–A short, creeping horror spurred by a postcard reprinting a 1919 invitation to a Physicians' Ball, illustrated with a skull and crossbones. Sometimes, the unexpected prompt can be the most fun.

"In Days of Auld Cheil's Crime"–2016 was a rough year for a lot of people in my sphere, never minding the cultural losses and other certain electoral incidents. At one point, I quipped the worst-case scenario would be 2016 killing and quietly taking the place of 2017 and simply continuing its reign of terror. The corruption of the new year and the conflicts of ancient gods grew organically from there. Also, I might have given 2016 a head full of bad ideas. Mea culpa.

"Bobby Boxster In Eight Measures"–In 2014, my good friend Keith clued me in to the Washington City Paper's annual Fiction Issue (seeking stories that captured the DC experience) and suggested I submit something. I'd already been in Houston four years at that point, but noodled some ideas. One, featuring Teddy Roosevelt's forgotten rail line out of DC, was a three-attempt non-starter. But I was reminded of a conversation I had Memorial Day 1999 in DC with a trumpeter outside Union Station. I'd first heard him playing "King of the Road" (that my friends call me the Road Warrior makes this only slightly more serendipitous in retrospect). He was playing for passing tourists and service members, we had a conversation, and I wound up writing a post about it for my at-the-time email column NOTHING'S SACRED. I hadn't really thought about the encounter for years before I started pondering a DC story. From the photo of his old combo in the case to his obvious skill to his rail-thin build and the depth of his gaze, most of the trappings of Bobby Boxster came from him. The fiction flowed from there.

"Withering"–I was musing online one afternoon about how it seemed so many touch-points of my life had vanished, consumed by the flow of time in unusual ways: my childhood home was renumbered out of existence by my home town; my grade school and high school had both closed, my college changed its name and tore down and replaced my dorm; almost every company I'd ever worked for had been acquired or gone out of business, on and on. I made a quip about being a "professional witherer" and was challenged by another writer to craft a story about such a thing, so I did. The postscript: in a life-imitates-art-imitates-that-kooky-observation-you-had moment, the story was purchased by BEYOND IMAGINATION, which published it as the final story in their final issue. The struggle is real, kids.

—o—

ACKNOWLEDGMENTS

Writing is an often-solitary pursuit; but the machinery of creation–sources of inspiration, moments of encouragement or constructive criticism, the birth and formation of ideas, the revision and strengthening of stories–is chock-a-block with trusted voices, critical thinkers, good friends, and wonderful souls who are in the right place at the right time to contribute a word, a notion, a pat on the back, or a dollop of praise. Thank you, thus, for one or all of the above, to:

Angela Antoniou; Keith Cramer; Jacquie Coven; Barney Dannelke; Mark Goldberg; Douglas Harrison; Michelle DeMarco; Harlan Ellison; Maureen Hall; Rick Keeney; David Leftwich; Melanie Martin; Sandra Odell; Jackie Olin; Maryanne Purtill; Shari Rosen; Jay Smith; Mary Stephens; Suresh Sundaram; Geri Trainham; and Kira Zalan.

Special thanks to my long-time collaborator, editor, science-corrector, and brother-by-another-mother, the Right Reverend Monseigneur Emeritus in Plenipotentiary Bernie Gaidasz, who's been playing narrative "what-if" with me for over 30 years.

And perpetual thanks, copious affection, and stupid amounts of love to my beautiful bride Peggy, for her love, patience, support, and willingness to put up with my muse when I'm called at 4 AM to write and don't come back to bed because I'm in the groove. It's not easy to love a writer, and harder to be loved by one. She handles both sides with uncommon grace.

ABOUT THE AUTHOR

Doug Lane's work has appeared in a broad range of publications and in nine languages (ten if you count the online bootleg Chinese translation of a screenplay he co-authored.) He dabbles in fantasy, science fiction, horror, and regular old lit-fiction. He's currently working on the third mystery novel in a series. His primary goal is to tell you a story. His secondary goal is for you to tell all your friends to read them.

Born in upstate New York, later of Northern Virginia, he currently resides in Houston, TX with his wife and their feline overlord. Visit www.douglasjlane.com or follow his ongoing adventures on Facebook (Doug Lane Writes) or occasionally Twitter (DougLaneWrites).

www.ingramcontent.com/pod-product-compliance
Lightning Source LLC
Chambersburg PA
CBHW020612120726
47905CB00003B/770